WHAT YOU LEFT ME

BRIDGET MORRISSEY

sourcebooks
fire

Published by Sourcebooks Fire, an imprint of Sourcebooks, Inc.
P.O. Box 4410, Naperville, Illinois 60567-4410
(630) 961-3900
Fax: (630) 961-2168
sourcebooks.com

Library of Congress Cataloging-in-Publication Data

Names: Morrissey, Bridget, author.
Title: What you left me / Bridget Morrissey.
Description: Naperville, Illinois : Sourcebooks Fire, [2018] | Summary: After four years of passing in the halls, Petra and Martin meet at graduation then, when a car accident puts Martin in a coma, Petra is left to keep the connection going in hopes he will awaken.
Identifiers: LCCN 2017046008
Subjects: | CYAC: Interpersonal relations--Fiction. | Coma--Fiction.
Classification: LCC PZ7.1.M675 Wh 2018 | DDC [Fic]--dc23 LC record available at https://lccn.loc.gov/2017046008

Printed and bound in the United States of America.
VP 10 9 8 7 6 5 4 3 2 1

For Mom and Dad

WHAT YOU LEFT ME

PART ONE

1

R ight here in the middle, with 867 other sweaty kids herded like cattle around me, I want to die. End it all on the football field. Burn up into ash and leave behind this hideous robe. There's no way I'm spending my afterlife wearing yellow polyester.

The first thing I did when I walked out here today was make an official announcement to everyone in my general vicinity. "In this gown, I am a disgrace to the McGee family name," I said.

I can't have my classmates thinking I don't know how ridiculous I look. I know, okay?

I know.

I'm not the most ridiculous person here though. That award goes to our valedictorian, Steve Taggart. There's no refund on the six minutes of my life I'm currently donating to his speech about how we're all birds taking flight. Dude, I'm not a bird. I'm

Martin McGee. I'm hot, I'm bored, and I don't have anyone to talk to right now. Forgive me while my eyes glaze over as I drift off into oblivion.

If I counted, and I mean if I got really specific, I'd say I know about four hundred of the people graduating today. That's including, like, the drug dealer who sits at my study hall table, that super tall blond who has a cross-country picture on the wall by the main entrance, and the girl who threw up before picture day in first grade. I don't see any of them right now. Based on the amount of random people around me, this could straight up be my first day of school.

Okay, maybe I don't want to die, but I could go for teleportation. I'd find Spits and talk him out of our bet. When this is all over, I'll need my ten bucks for a celebratory meal. It's the only money I have to my name, and, well, high school will be done.

That calls for a sandwich.

......

Oh, Steve Taggart. Sweat has painted circles through his yellow robe. The random smattering of claps that follow his final sentence must be more for his underarm artwork than his terrible speech. My personal applause is for the end of Steve Taggart's reign as smartest kid in school. See you in hell, Steve Taggart! Or at Notre Dame, but maybe the universe will grant me one kindness and make it so we never cross paths there.

At the rate I'm going, it won't be a problem.

Steve walks back to his spot, smug and sweat-drenched, and

settles into the innermost aisle seat of the front row. The rest of the top ten sit alongside him in order of class rank. The chosen ones.

I'm in the miserable middle, plain old Petra McGowan of the *M* section, sandwiched between my alphabetical neighbors. Three different middle schools merged into our high school, and while there are faces nearby that I've known my whole life, there are also faces I swear I've never seen before. Like the two complete strangers on either side of me. For four years, we've coexisted, sharing walls and desks and hall passes and gossip without ever managing to cross paths. When you try hard to be good at this whole school thing, you end up with the same group of people in every class. As the years tick by, the numbers dwindle. No one ever randomly decides to take an AP course. This is the first and only time we've all been united; a bunch of squirming and vibrating cells being observed by the microscope that is the high-noon sun, waiting for this pomp and circumstance to end.

Steve Taggart's speech marks the end of one part of the ceremony and the beginning of the next—the ever-important receipt of the diploma. It begins with the parade of our most intelligent: Valedictorian Steve, Salutatorian Marissa Huang, third in the class Jay Cattaro, and then, my favorite mouthful of a name, Cameron Catherine Elizabeth Hannafin-Bower.

Cameron's wiry auburn hair engulfs her profile until she becomes nothing but a moving ball of energy, all warm colors and excited twitches. She turns to face the crowd and flashes her most vibrant gap-toothed smile at me. Or in my general vicinity. I'm not sure she can see this far back. Rank eleventh like me, and there is no fanfare. You're deep among the plebeians, permanently imprinting your lower half into a foldout plastic chair while waiting for your spot in the alphabet.

At least I was blessed with McGowan for a last name, not Prabhu or Stetson. Poor Aminah and Daniel. It'll be hours before they get to graduate. *P* and *S* may not seem very far from me, but I'm almost positive a third of our graduating glass has an *M* last name.

Mister tenth in the class—the last of the spots that could have been mine if things had been different—walks across the stage, ending the stream of academic overachievers getting their only moment of priority over the athletes.

How nice it would've been to get that single candle flicker of justice.

The march of the mundane begins with Alex Abraham. His mom breaks the rules and uses a blow horn when his name is called, sending a much-needed jolt of energy through our class. The boy next to me jumps out of his seat.

······

Alex Abraham's mom uses a blow horn. I jump out of my seat.

"Aw, c'mon," I say to myself. And kind of to the girl next to me. She turns a little, brushing a piece of her hair out of her eyes to see me, so I keep going. "Alex Abraham's gotta be angling for some kind of last-ditch recognition as a rebel or something. I swear I've never heard that kid say more than five words in my whole life. Now he's got the family bringing out blow horns? Let it go, kid. It's over."

The girl does something halfway between laughing and shrugging. We aren't supposed to talk, but it's a rule without consequence. It's not like they'll take away our diplomas now.

I pass time by trying to list every Cubs manager I can recall, in reverse chronological order. I'm all the way back to Leo Durocher (1966–1972), when I catch sight of Spits shuffling into his seat. He's arrived right in between the graduations of Bryant Carpenter and Eduardo Carrera, and he's causing a tiny commotion while making his way down his row. The other graduates yelp as he trips over their feet. Spits just laughs.

"He's such a loser," I mutter, half laughing to myself.

"I'll say," the girl next to me quips back.

I'm stunned. I shoot her a look, but she's got her eyes right back on her hands, the smallest trace of a smile hanging on her lips.

A paper airplane crashes into the lap of the dude on my other side, who has somehow managed to stay asleep through the horn blowing. Good for him. I look around for a culprit—it's Spits of course, his metal mouth on full display, grinning like he took a hit seconds before and is riding the high. Classic. He points to the airplane.

bet you can't get that girl next to you to come tonight.
also get my ten bucks ready.

—spitty

"Wanna hear something funny?" I ask the girl. Might as well make one last friend before I dance across the stage, grab my damn diploma, and keg stand my way into a victorious summer. "My buddy, uh, Spencer, bet me ten bucks that my mom will yell out Marty McFly when they call my name."

"Why would she do that?"

"Because my name's Martin McGee."

"Then who is Marty McFly?"

"You have to know who Marty McFly is."

"A sports guy?"

My laugh is the blow horn now. It scares her. "Come to my party tonight," I say. "I'll lend you *Back to the Future*."

"Where's it at?" she asks. It looks like one of her cheeks gets red, but it's hard to tell when she's facing the other direction. Her hair's curled in that way all girls seem to do for special occasions, pieces of it twisted like coiled ribbons around her head. She wraps one strand around her finger until it becomes a perfect brown spiral.

"My place," I tell the girl. "Mama Dorothy lets me use our basement for parties. Everyone has to put their car keys in a bowl and promise to spend the night if they drink. I live right behind the school." I point toward the trees beyond the field. "Ugly orange house with a basketball hoop in the driveway. You can't miss it."

"Cool," she says. She puts her hands in her lap and starts chipping off the sparkly stuff on her nails.

......

This whole ordeal is supposed to be my last punishment, closing up shop on the era that will someday be known as *the time Petra just graduated.* Emphasis on the word *just*, as if plain graduation is a disease to be contracted, because there isn't anything to follow it with, such as *in the top ten*, like my sister Jessica, or even better, *as the valedictorian*, like my sister Caroline.

Just graduated.

But here's Martin McGee. Interrupting me.

"Gotta kill the time," he says, "or this thing is gonna kill me." He has the delivery of a stand-up comedian, every word crackling with extra flair so that no sentence sounds ordinary.

"I hear you," I respond, wiping away the newest beads of sweat forming along my hairline. I spent half an hour curling my hair just right, and the heat has been trying its hardest to undo all my work.

Our principal cuts in front of the man reciting the names. "In the interest of time, we ask that everyone refrain from making any noises for the remainder of the ceremony. Thank you."

Someone boos in an act of defiance.

"Wow. Gotta love this town," Martin mutters under his breath.

I've never understood why you're supposed to feel this unfounded disdain for where you come from, as if it is the unclassiest, most smothering place that ever existed. "I like it just fine," I say to him.

"You might be the first."

We go quiet again.

......

Spits makes faces at me. *You failed*, he mouths, smiling of course, and pointing to the girl, who's kind of pretending to ignore me by leaning forward and staring at the grass. I wad up the note and try to throw it at Spits, but it bounces off the head of someone who doesn't even react.

"My friend over there told me to invite you to my party. He thinks I failed," I say to the girl.

"How? You already invited me."

"Failing would be you not showing up."

"How does he know that I won't go?"

"Exactly. Orange house. Basketball hoop. Ten o'clock."

"We'll see."

"Who are you?"

"The name next to yours in the yearbook," she says.

I try to get a good look at her, but the sun's so bright she becomes her own kind of light. Her eyes are all I can make out. They're brown, but a shiny kind, like maple syrup glistening on a pancake.

Man, I'm hungry.

"Guess I need to pay better attention to the yearbook," I say.

"Same," she whispers.

......

When I open my mouth to speak, my voice crackles with Martin's style of speech, one so easy to fall into, I do it without even realizing. My dress may as well be made of concrete. It blocks my exasperated air from releasing, shoving it into space around my rib cage.

"We've got a whole list of things to do," he says. "Number one, watch *Back to the Future.* I can't sleep until you've met the real Marty McFly."

"You know I can stream it, right?"

"You can?" His tone isn't mocking, just playful. "My copy is special though. It's the Marty 'Fly' McGee platinum edition. Extremely rare. Actually, one of a kind."

"Wow. What an honor."

"Please, please. It's not a big deal. I don't like to make a fuss. At the end of the day, I'm just a regular guy."

We share a laugh. As it tapers out, there's a pause, like in the space between words, something has shifted. It's almost awkward.

Martin swoops back in to save the moment. "All right, back to my list. Number two, look at our yearbook. If I've missed you, my alphabetical neighbor I've never been put next to at any other school thing, who knows what else might be in there?" He pauses to smile at me. Mouth open, molars visible, so lacking in self-consciousness that I have to bite the inside of my cheek to keep myself from smiling too big in return. "Number three, I'm gonna need you to show me what there is to love about this place." He takes out his phone. "So, Graduation Girl, how about a phone number for your new friend Marty McGee?"

I shake my head no, because if there is one lesson I will take away from my four years here, one definitive thing I have learned, the hard way, it is to beware the smiling sweet talker.

Stop while you're ahead, Petra.

You have more important things to accomplish this weekend.

......

Graduation Girl's got her own set of tricks. No name. Won't give me her number. Smells like that fancy soap store in the mall where all the girls get their bath bombs. "Seriously though, how have we never met?" I ask her.

Ms. Hornsby, resident terrifying math teacher, walks by to shush us. Graduation Girl gets all flustered, which makes me laugh. "What can she do to us for talking?" GG doesn't answer. "I've got a lot of bucket list items to cross off with you," I say, trying to puff out my voice so it sounds bigger. More confident.

"Martin!" Ms. Hornsby scolds. "Be quiet!"

"Yeah, Martin," GG jokes, "be quiet." She plays it like she's kidding, but I can tell she means it. Her chipped-off nail polish is all over the lap of her gown, and she's going to town on the little that is left on her nails.

My mind runs through all the ways I could get her to notice me again. There's always flicking her arm. Eh. Being annoying doesn't seem like the right move. I look around for another idea and accidentally make hard eye contact with Hornsby, which makes me sweat, which makes me overcompensate, which makes me start humming, which is actually the perfect solution. It's not talking. It's fair game.

After a big throat clear and a good neck crack, I push air through my teeth to recreate the synthesized greatness of Van Halen. No human being can resist the musical mastery that is "Jump."

I check in on Graduation Girl. The ridiculousness of my humming should be at least a half smile's worth of points from her.

Nope. She is stone-faced. Royal guards would be jealous.

I amp up my effort, hammering the song's rhythm into my leg and humming louder. I did choir in grade school, so I know I'm nailing my pitches (boy sopranos represent!), but the end of the introduction is nearing, and the magic of the music doesn't seem to be affecting her. Still, I hit the final majestic synth high notes, burying my head into my neck to give the kind of commitment the song deserves, and *sweet-holy-patron-saint-of-Cubs-baseball-Ernie-Banks,* I catch sight of movement on the ground.

It's her foot. Tapping along.

Like David Lee Roth and Sammy Hagar and every other random lead singer they've had, she comes in for the first line. "*Dog it off,*" she sings under her breath. The rest comes out as an incoherent mumble.

The lyrics are so wrong I almost keel over and die laughing. I decide to bring my other hand in for a better drum section instead. This is too good to stop. GG takes over the humming, and I pick up the next line of the song (with the correct lyrics, of course) as if we planned it this way all along. We look at each other, her pounding the beat into the grass and me into my legs, and we sing together until we get to the chorus's lead-in. Graduation Girl hits me with the most ridiculously wrong lyrics of all time, but she is one hundred percent committed to the feeling. When it comes time to speak the line before the chorus, I say it all cool, and then she echoes back the title with perfect timing, shouting it with the exact amount of power and feeling required. She throws her head back and laughs at herself. It's like an ad for shampoo the way her hair falls over the edge of her chair, all long and curly and flowing.

"Shut up!" the no-longer-sleeping guy on the other side of me whisper-yells.

Graduation Girl and I laugh louder. "My dad loves that song," she whispers, catching her volume. "We always just make up the words as we go."

"I can tell," I say. "My dad loves it too. Official postseason anthem for the 1984 Cubs, baby. Big ups to two of the all-time greats, Rick Sutcliffe and Ryne Sandberg. Love you, Rick and Ryno." I pat my chest and then blow a kiss to the Rick and Ryne in my head.

Ms. Hornsby pulls her finger to her mouth and gives the loudest shush ever known to man. Graduation Girl straightens up.

......

This is outrageous. Four years of high school have come and gone without a single sighting of Martin McGee, now here we are singing our respective fathers' favorite eighties rock anthem together on the football field. Ms. Hornsby has threatened to remove Martin from the ceremony if he speaks again. He's mostly obeying. Just nudging me and tapping my foot with his.

I can feel my head getting lighter, pulling me out of my seat and into the clouds, loosening the anchor at the bottom of my stomach. I'm fighting for gravity. Fighting to stop my mind from wandering and wondering about this kid that's been one name away from me all this time.

Come on, Petra. Stay ahead.

You cannot piss off Ms. Hornsby now.

......

I play games on my phone to get Hornsby to leave me alone. I'd love to see her try and kick me out of here, but it's more entertaining to sit next to Graduation Girl. We communicate through elbow nudges and impatient foot shaking. Sometimes you don't need to speak to have a conversation.

After a long while, my fingers get so hot from the sun beating down and my phone's battery working overtime that I put it back in my pocket. Graduation Girl eyes me. It'll be worth it to get kicked out if I can just get her number. Hell, even her name. "Hey," I say.

She glares at me.

"I know. I know." I knock it down to a whisper. "What if we played a game? You give me three letters of the alphabet to guess from, one of which is the first letter of your name. If I get it right in less than thirty tries, you have to come to my party."

"That sounds like a terrible game." This girl cuts no corners.

"You're right. It does." I nudge her shoulder. "At least I'm not our valedictorian, out here talking about how we're all baby birds ready to leave the nest."

"Did you watch his nose when he spoke?" She sounds kind of mischievous when she asks. Clearly, I've chosen a solid topic.

"Can't say I was paying much attention to his nose, no. Why?"

"His nostrils always do this flapping thing every time he breathes."

It's not what I'm expecting her to say. I belly laugh. She wraps her hand around my forearm in a vice grip to silence me. "I'm sorry," I whisper, almost breaking. "How did you even notice that?"

"Steve Taggart is my archnemesis," she answers in the most deadpan whisper I've ever heard. "Knowing everything about him used to be my life's mission."

She's so close I can smell her again; this flowery, honey scent is wafting right up into my nostrils. I'm glad she seems to refuse to ever look at me because I might be doing the Steve Taggart thing too without even knowing it. "I think I need to make it my life's mission to know more about you." I say it before realizing how much it sounds like a terrible line. I didn't mean it to be that way.

More than anything, I want to be her friend. And I want her to want *me* as a friend.

Still, it backfires. She balls up into her seat and starts picking at her nail polish again. The sun becomes so instantly and unbearably hot I have to loosen my tie.

Dammit. I can never get it right when it counts.

......

It needed to end. There is no room in my life for a boy like Martin McGee. Not even as a friend. It would just be another distraction. I'm already well stocked.

Ms. Hornsby walks by and slips me a satisfied smirk, as if she knows I've just gone cold turkey on Martin. He must be trouble. Is every boy trouble? My vision blurs at the thought.

Names drone on. People graduate. The world keeps spinning, even when I push against it, trying to set it back the other way.

······

Graduation Girl's presence is a force. I wonder if she knows that. She's not doing a single thing, barely even breathing it seems, and still it feels like she controls time itself. Right now, it stalls for her. The announcer guy reads in slow motion gibberish. Kids walk across the stage like their legs are sticks and the ground is mud. In my head, I go back to listing Cubs managers, and I swear I almost make it all the way to the late 1800s before another minute passes.

Then, like a finger snap, she sets the world back on track with one sentence. "Isn't that your friend?"

Spitty's waving at me, pointing to his wrist. Like he's ever worn a watch in his life. Once I acknowledge him, he starts pretending to chug and toss imaginary liquor bottles. *Your ten-dollar bill is mine, bitch*, he mouths. His smile is an explosion of metal fireworks.

"Best one I've ever had," I say to Graduation Girl.

"Is it wrong for me to hope you win this bet?" Her voice is so soft I have to piece the sentence together afterward. She's looking everywhere but me, trying to see if Hornsby is watching us.

"I'd never tell you how to feel," I crack off. "But you're on the right side of this battle, for sure."

"Well, I'd never feel the way you told me to, anyway."

"Good."

"Perfect."

"Great."

"Prodigious."

Out of nowhere, Hornsby pops up. This woman is every-where. She looks right at Graduation Girl. "You really can't afford to be making so much trouble right now. I can only do so much," she tells her.

"I have no idea what *prodigious* even means," I say when Hornsby's gone.

Graduation Girl doesn't acknowledge me. She's slunk down so low into her robe she's almost a turtle. It doesn't even make sense. Hornsby just treated her like high school still matters. And Graduation Girl is acting like Hornsby is right about that. But we're *at* graduation. It's very confusing.

Graduation Girl doesn't say or do anything until it's our turn to stand up and graduate, no matter how many times I clear my throat or pretend to notice something really interesting in the sky or the grass or next to my foot or whatever.

Our favorite *shush*ing teacher motions for our aisle to rise and start walking toward the podium. I do a big stretch and let out a yawn, hoping Graduation Girl will react. We're on the move. Maybe she won't feel so bad about talking now?

After my fourth time twisting my torso back and forth like I'm preparing to run a marathon, Graduation Girl sighs. "You are ridiculous," she says.

"Come to my party. Please."

Graduation Girl doesn't answer. Instead—and I didn't know this was a thing real humans did, I've only ever seen it in movies—her eyes flutter, like she's batting her damn lashes. She laughs a private little laugh that loops in my head like a victory song. Of course *her* yellow robe has turned her into the Sunshine Statue of Liberty. She seems powerful and serene and a little sad, which is probably exactly what Lady Liberty feels like posted up all by herself in the water. I realize she's standing in front of Brittany McMahon. I forgot I know Brittany McMahon. She's one of those people who makes you go, "Oh yeah, you. You were in my day care back in the day, weren't you?"

We start walking down the aisle. The dry grass of the football field is pressed flat from all the people before us. As we make our single-file line on the left side of the podium, I look out into the crowd to try and spot Spitty or Turrey or, hell, even Chris, but no one's paying attention to anything. It's like boredom is an actual disease, and everyone is a couple of breaths away from dying of it. I put my head down and stare at my kicks, looking fresh and ready for their official graduation debut. Getting the chance to put them on this morning was one of the only things that got me out of bed. I'd say they're the only things I care about right now, but if I'm being honest with myself, this Graduation Girl has my head kind of spinning.

I refocus myself by limbeing up for my planned dance across the stage. Spits was supposed to dance too, but he chickened out. I knew he would. He walked across like he was balancing a book on his head, all proud, acting the part of Spencer Alan Kuspits Jr. I should've bet money he'd do that. Then I wouldn't lose my ten bucks.

17

The sleepy guy before me goes across to dead silence. Good. I'll spice it up. Mama Dorothy doesn't know what quiet means. Two of my aunts are here, and they're super loud. Then there's my sister Katie and her husband, and I swear they get paid to be professional sports fans. They're always at some game or another. They're going to be screaming.

"Martin Frederick McGee."

I walk up the three steps in total silence. I'm going to win the bet with Spits. I don't want to win the bet anymore. I want to lose my ten dollars. I want to make Graduation Girl laugh again.

I look up into the bleachers to find my family. They're starting to stand, with posters in hand. *I love you Marty McFly!* yells Mama Dorothy.

Phew.

Everyone holds a different letter. *M-C-F-Y-L-!* My aunts look at each other and switch spots. *M-C-F-L-Y-!* My sister puts down her letter and holds up her phone. The version of "Fly Like An Eagle" they use in the movie *Space Jam* starts playing, and I'll be damned if that song doesn't make me believe I can. I run in slow motion toward my diploma, airplane wings on and a dramatic spin here and there, just like the singer Seal would want.

Damn. Guess Taggart is right. I *am* a bird.

GG stands at the steps, waiting to cross after me. As I spin, I catch her cupping her mouth, a smile showing at the corners.

Success.

......

Martin McGee surely went out how he went in, a funny dude skating by on wild antics, always going over the top for the joke, never passing up an opportunity to make an impression. He shoots me a wink. I can't help but laugh. This boy. He really does seem so good. Can it be true? Do they exist?

Against my better judgment, the corners of my mouth stay pulled upward. Nothing will get my face to calm down, not scolding or biting my cheek or the thought of algebraic equations.

"Petra Margaret McGowan."

That sobers me right up.

I step up the stairs. An almost serene silence accompanies me, allowing me to hear every meaningless thank-you from the faculty members as we shake hands. The last one gives me my empty diploma holder. Everything I've ever worked for, my entire life really, is now represented by one missing eight-and-a-half-by-eleven sheet of cardstock. It's all been for the very piece of paper I don't yet have. The anchor in my stomach scrapes along my intestines as it sinks deeper. I'd be stuck standing in the middle of the stage for the rest of my life if not for the simple, powerful fact that no other graduate knows this black folder is empty. To them, I am just a girl in the middle of the class. I smile and smile and smile and smile until I'm down the steps on the other side of the stage.

I'd always pictured this whole thing ending here, as if I could throw my cap in the air and head straight to a painful family dinner at Olive Garden. But it isn't over when I walk across the stage. It's over when all 868 students walk across the stage.

I'm merely the halfway point. So back into the line I go, en route to my assigned seat, my leaden legs propelled forward by the promise of seeing Martin again. He's there, cheesing like someone's let him in on the best, most exciting secret known to man.

"Petra, Petra, Petra," he says when I walk down. "Petra riding the Metra. You betcha, Petra."

"So you know my name now," I say with an eye roll, mostly because making any kind of real eye contact with him seems deadlier than the boredom afflicting every student within a fifty-mile radius of this football field.

"Not just your first name. I know your *whole* name." He taps the boy in front of him on the shoulder. "Excuse me, man, I just wanted you to know that this girl here is my best friend, Petra Margaret McGowan. Petty Margs, I call her. I know you heard our singing earlier. I think our music's so good we just might start a band with that name."

"Dude, get over yourself," the boy says as he shrugs off Martin's touch.

Martin tosses a half grin my way. "This guy clearly doesn't know classic rock like we do, Petty Margs."

"I can't with you."

"No one can."

We're waiting for the rest of our row to graduate so we can walk back to our seats in, quote, "uniform fashion." With every name called, I remind myself to breathe. I'm supposed to be sulking. This is supposed to be torture. But it isn't. No matter what I do, I can't shake the Martin McGee I'm wearing all over my mood.

......

I'm supposed to be bored. This is supposed to be torture. But it isn't. There's a Petra Margaret McGowan–size light shining on me, and it's brighter than anything the sun is trying to make happen up in the sky right now.

Wow. I can be cheesy.

Whatever. I own it.

It's so strange though because I can't even remember the last time I felt this charged up. Maybe when I tried to get Holly Paulson to go to the seventh-grade dance with me. My sister Katie and I stayed up all night making a shoe box diorama of Holly and I holding each other on the dance floor. I had to carry it with me the entire school day because the only class I had with Holly was my last one. By the time it rolled around, she'd already heard about the box from everybody else, so there was all this expectation, and when we finally saw each other, neither of us really knew how to go about it all. I ended up saying nothing and just handing her the diorama as if that was enough. She looked at me like I'd shown up to school in just my underwear, because the project featured Popsicle stick people with our school pictures pasted onto their heads.

It's like that—like I'm holding an obvious question but unsure how to really ask it. My words are glue, stuck inside my mouth.

Oh, and Holly said no, by the way. So there's that too.

......

Somehow, Martin and I get stuck in a silence so weighted it lassoes around my throat. Something between us got lost up on the stage. Or maybe found. It's hard to tell with all the loaded silence blocking my peripherals. I study the intricate details of my yellow robe, distracting myself by imagining what it might be to finally, maybe, let myself like a boy again. Why are ceremonies practically designed for this kind of introspection? It's as unavoidable as the brightness all around me.

Ryan Hales emerges, like a light that's been turned on in the attic of my mind. The squareness of his face, so symmetrical that you could slice him down the middle and come up with mirror images. He's rubbing his hands on his jeans, asking me on a date in front of my locker. His hands stop when I say yes. He's kicking the rocks outside of the tennis courts, waiting to give me a ride home, stopping when I walk up. Tossing my homework out the window when I tell him I have too much, stopping when I panic.

We're in the back seat of his car. Sweat is pouring down my back.

"Your eyes look like pancakes," Martin says finally, after what could be years or milliseconds. He dissolves Ryan into nothing more than a mirage I never meant to chase.

"What?" It's such an absurd sentiment that my laughter doesn't feel like too much of a giveaway. *I'm laughing* at *Martin, not with him*, I assure myself. And laughter is a great distraction from the aftershock of surfacing memories.

"I mean maple syrup," he corrects.

I still don't let myself look at him, but the heat radiating from his cheeks burns stronger than the sun. I can't help but soften. "Petty Margs and the Maple Syrup Eyes. Our official band name."

Out of the corner of my eye, I see his shoulders relax. "Available for weddings, birthdays, and graduations."

Ms. Hornsby signals for us to walk back to our seats. I stare at my feet as we start moving, thinking about everything and nothing at once. When I look back up, Martin is nowhere to be found.

......

Sneaking out had no unforeseen difficulties. Zig when everyone zags. Easy as that. Spits waits for me behind the bleachers. He pulls two travel-size bottles of whiskey out from beneath his robe and hands one to me.

"Cheers!" he says.

We chug them back in one gulp.

Don't know where I'm going next, but I like the way everything looks right now. A little too bright and way too hot, but exactly the way I want it to be. High school took my sobriety and most of my dignity, so Spits and I break our whiskey bottles on the bleacher mud to honor all we gave to this sacred ground.

"You look nice," Spits says, tugging on the part of my tie he can see above my robe. "Now give me my ten bucks."

"Take it and use it for the greater good," I tell him, shaking off the nagging feeling that I've left behind something essential. "Beer would be very appreciated at the McGee residence tonight," I say as Spits lifts up his robe and crams my ten-dollar bill down his pants. "You're sick, you know that?"

"Shut up. Let's go for one last joy ride before this thing ends. I promise we'll be back in time for your mom to give me a big kiss, and you know she will." He tries to click his heels together but gets tripped up on his robe. "Shut up!" he yells, but I'm already laughing.

Spitty and I arrive at his parking spot. I usually keep my crying reserved for baseball games and videos of pets being reunited with owners, but I'd be lying if I said the sight of his raggedy Dodge Caravan didn't choke me up. "I thought you were driving with your dad."

"Did you want me to bring him to the liquor store? *Hold on, Pop. Grabbing some whiskey for me and Fly.* He drove himself. I rode solo in the White Whale."

I climb in. The passenger seat is pushed and leaned back to my exact preference, covered in stains and nostalgia. I am the co-king of the White Whale. This is my throne.

Spits takes out two more baby whiskeys. We chug, so fast I get a bubble caught in my throat, then toss the little bottles out the White Whale's manual windows, cranking the handles as fast as we can to let in the fresh air. Spitty takes a hard left out of the school lot. Not a car in sight.

"By the way," I say, grabbing at the warm summer air as it flies through my fingers. "That girl's coming tonight." I smile at the thought of Petra, imagining her walking through my front door, eyes shooting left to right, scanning for me.

Me.

Accelerating speed pulls my cheeks back. I can almost taste the future's possibilities in the wind whooshing through my mouth.

......

No one cares about Martin's empty seat. No one checks. Rules are gone, because for 867 other people, high school is officially over.

I could throw up.

Without him here, I remember the reason for my initial dread. Every reason, actually. Every twelve-hour school day. Every agonizing assignment. Every painstaking triumph and hard-earned grade. My years of work all erased, obsolete, rendered irrelevant. Because of one misstep, none of it matters. None of it pays off.

At some point, the ceremony ends, and I hear, "Congratulations, graduates!" At some point, I switch over my tassel and rise up to toss my cap into the air. Doing what Dad's always asked of me. Faking it until I make it, even though I know it's not that simple.

At some point, families crowd the football field.

At some point, Cameron finds me. "We did it!" she squeals, as if there were ever a question in her mind that we would.

If only she knew...

"We're going to a party tonight," I tell her. A surprised look smushes her freckles into the wrinkled creases on her nose.

Martin McGee, I will find you again.

2

I f there's a light switch to be found, I can't reach it.

I can't do anything at all.

It isn't darkness, but it isn't light. It's gray without being gray because you can see gray, and this can't be seen. Or felt. Or tasted or smelled or heard.

It just is.

......

My entire uncelebratory dinner at Olive Garden, while Caroline and Jessica reminisced about their high school days and my parents listened with wistful fondness, I tried to remember the last party I attended. Cameron and I did a campus visit together last fall. We had different hosts inside the same dorm, and they invited us to an off-campus thing. We stayed for all of twenty minutes before we were over it.

I trudged back further into the recesses of my memory—the darker places—and I came up with something more relevant. Summer before junior year, I went to a bonfire. I had two sips of lukewarm beer from a red cup and left before eleven. That had to be carefully excavated out of a pile of much more substantial memories with Ryan Hales. Just above the first time we met and below the first time we held hands. And even those I strained to recall, mostly because I get a vinegar taste in my mouth whenever I think of him.

Martin's party stands for something different. It's the end of an era while managing to be the beginning too. It's the last shred of high school cocktailed with whatever we're heading into now.

......

This sounds so impossible, but I know I have my brain. I'm thinking these thoughts right now; I must have my brain. It's just that I can't find my body.

It's not freaking me out. It should be, but it's not. There's nowhere to process the freaking out of things.

There is nowhere.

......

"Wear shoes you can walk in," Cameron reminds Aminah as she peruses my closet for a pair that matches her tank top.

"It might surprise you, but I can figure that out on my own," Aminah claws back.

Cameron opens my backpack and pulls out my yearbook. "All

right, Martin McGee, let's see who you are." She turns one page back and forth repeatedly, her face twisted into a confused snarl. "He should be right before you."

"Check the Not Pictured section," Aminah chimes in, all the while settling on a pair of white sandals identical to ones she already owns. She catches me giving her an odd look. "Yours are in better condition," she tells me, as if confessing.

"Weird. It says he's not pictured. What's that about? Let's see if he was in any clubs," Cameron says.

"Or sports," Aminah adds.

"Right."

I curl up next to Cameron for investigation, disappointed to discover that Martin McGee does not exist in photo form.

"Why aren't we checking Instagram?" Aminah asks. "Petra's talking about a boy. This is a first since—" She stops and picks up a lip gloss, pretending to be bored by her slipup.

Ryan is home from his first year of college, and it's like everyone can feel it. He's an invisible weight slipping into any crevice he can find, making even the smallest of talk seem heavy.

"I told Daniel to meet us there," Aminah says as an answer to a question no one asked, moving the conversation away from her error.

We head toward my front door. My mom is half asleep on the couch.

"Have you looked at your study—" my mom starts to ask.

I close the door before Aminah and Cameron can hear the end of her sentence.

"Tomorrow," I call out to her from the other side. "It's nothing," I say to my friends. "Just college stuff."

The truth is an art form.

......

It's like I'm stuck on the inside of a blink. The first one after a long night of sleep, when your eyes don't really open. It's just a flutter of moving grayness, but you know something is happening on the other side of your lids—the start of a new day.

Do I see this?

Am I feeling it?

What does something become when it's all there seems to be?

......

We walk down dark side streets elbow to elbow.

"We graduated!" Aminah shouts.

I should tell them what's going on with me. But I can't.

I can't.

Cameron nudges me, seeking shared acknowledgment of Aminah's flair for the dramatic. It used to be Aminah who led our smart-girl group. Cameron and I admired her, strived to be her, studied extra hours to reach her heights of intelligence. Then junior year came, and Aminah surrendered her title without explanation, swapping out impossible academic standards for personal liberation. All we knew was that she seemed happier. That was what mattered.

"What a perfect way to kick off our last summer together,"

Aminah reflects, nuzzling Cameron and me in for a walking hug. "We are women now!"

Cameron lets out a single laugh, her patented indication to Aminah that she's being ridiculous. "We've always been women."

Cameron, being the thorough girl that she is, vacuumed up every bit of neuroses Aminah shed junior year. She wears it in her attitude, always selective with the moments she allows to get the best of her.

"No. Before, we were girls. Now, real life begins!"

They settle into quarreling without so much as a breath in my direction.

Aminah and Cameron have been the same since kindergarten. Aminah might be freer and Cameron might be more neurotic, but at their core, they've always been a perfectly complementary pair. I've always felt like the wild card when it comes to the three of us. Even in appearance. My skin tans easily but turns sallow in winter. My hair was blond when I was younger and has since browned. It used to be curly, now I have to do it with an iron. The rounded puff of my cheeks deflates with every passing year. Of course, the way we appear does not dictate all of who we are to one another, but it's hard not to notice that while Aminah and Cameron look like someone digitally age-progressed their grade school photos—adding occasionally used glasses on Cameron around eighth grade and braces on Aminah from ninth to tenth—I'm unrecognizable most of the time.

Even to myself.

"I think we turn here," I contribute in the midst of their arguing. They pivot in unison.

In the center of a cul-de-sac, flanked by identical ranch houses, sits a two-level orange anomaly with a basketball hoop in front. The home is a statement piece straight from the 1970s, complete with a yellow security light casting eerie horror film shadows on the rusting clapboard.

"No lights on inside."

"Probably because everyone's in the basement."

"Where'd they all park?"

"If they're drinking, maybe they walked like we did?" Cameron guesses.

"Wow. Please never again assume that the rest of our graduating class is anywhere near as responsible as you are," Aminah shoots back.

"Should I knock?" I ask.

Aminah takes her cell phone out of her bra. "Let me call Daniel."

She brings the phone to her ear, and I peek in a window, looking for signs of life.

"Hey, are you here?" A long pause. "What do you mean?" She puts her hand over the phone and looks at me. "Does he go by Fly?"

"What?"

"This guy hosting the party. Is his nickname Fly?"

"I don't know. He said his mom calls him Marty McFly."

"Daniel's saying he got in a car accident after graduation. No one knows anything for sure, but people are saying he could be dead."

......

I know I graduated today.

I ate a sesame bagel with jalapeños and extra cream cheese this morning.

Drank three forties with Spits, Turrey, and Chris two nights ago.

Got in another fight with Brooke after prom.

Skipped my last final.

Bought two bags of Cheetos, a roll of toilet paper, and a case of Keystone Light at the end of last week.

During the ceremony, I swear I struggled for a second to remember Spits's real name. He's been Spits or Spitty as long as I've been Marty or Fly, which is as long as I can remember. Now I can come up with the first time I knew he was going to be my best friend. Second-grade recess kickball game. Third inning, bases loaded. He caught my kick then dropped it because he saw I was about to cry, letting my team win the game. He had on khaki shorts with a hole where the left pocket should've been. You could see his Batman underwear. Everyone made fun of him for it. They called him Spitman for like the next three years.

This is all stuff I forgot. Even what I ate this morning. It was erased, and now it's here. It's all here. Except my body. And things to taste or see or smell or touch.

What did I do?

I got in the White Whale. I grabbed at the air, thinking of Graduation Girl. Then something pushed me. Pushed and pushed until I folded inside of myself.

3

Spencer's head hits the airbag over and over, the impact replaying on a loop. His thoughts repeat, too, locked on the first thing that comes to mind as another car barrels into the White Whale's passenger side.

Crash. Smack.

I killed my best friend.

It's the worst thought he's ever had.

Crash. Smack.

I killed my best friend.

It's the only thought he'll ever have again.

Time jumps forward. Sirens flash red. Blood bleeds red. The world tangles into a knot that cannot be untied.

Time jumps backward. Fresh air, so pure, flows into the van. Spencer presses harder on the gas pedal. His heel digs into the car mat beneath.

Martin opens his mouth to speak, but words won't form.

Time hiccups.

Crash. Smack.

I killed my best friend.

4

A huge chunk of our graduating class appears to be crowded into this waiting room, huddled in corners, draped over chairs, and banging on vending machines. Not a recognizable debate team, science club, ecology club, or honor society member in sight. I don't know anyone. I don't really know Martin either, but I'm here anyway, pulled in by fascination, regret, and avoidance in equal parts.

Everyone wears daytime formal attire, with some still in their yellow robes. Cameron, Aminah, and I look precisely casual. Bonfire chic. As if we need another way to stick out.

"We were texting this morning. It's so unreal," says a girl as she cries into her friend's gown sleeve. She passes her phone around for others to see. "Can you believe he wrote that? *You mean so much to me.* It's like he knew something bad would happen."

The phone ends up in my hands. I scroll up.

Thank you for a great year

Brooke don't do this

Why can't I say that?
Whatever.
Happy graduation
See you at the ceremony
Maybe

Brooke come on
You know how I feel
You mean so much to me
But don't ruin summer because of this
We can still be friends
Like before

"You're bad!" Aminah says, scrolling up even farther to read more.

"Come on, you guys, have some respect!" Cameron whispers, curt.

"She's the one passing it around!" Aminah whispers back.

Another person yanks the phone from Aminah, and we all cower a bit. Fear of reprimand. Nothing happens though. The girl who took the phone spends way more time looking it over than we did. She, like me, like everyone else, wants to know another side of Martin, Marty, Fly, whoever he is. Wants a good story to share years down the line, should it turn out that he really died on graduation day.

......

Whoa.

For a flicker, I was back in the White Whale with Spitty. It wasn't like here, where I'm in a blink, but it wasn't like real life either. Everything blurred and changed. Something crushed me, then rewound, then crushed again, then disappeared. Sound polluted my mind with buzzing and blaring and sobbing.

Then it was beautiful, sunny, and warm, and I grabbed at the air.

Then something crushed me again.

Every moment came and went as quick as a clap of hands. Too fast for me to process.

I know all of it happened to me, but it wasn't quite mine somehow. It was like I lived my part in it through someone else's—Spitty's?—perspective.

......

A man enters the waiting area. He's got a dad energy about him—the oversize polo tucked into shorts is the big giveaway—but he's not sad enough to be Martin's dad. Judging by the little I know of Martin, I imagine his dad would have to be like Jim Carrey when he did all those serious movies that my oldest sister Caroline loves so much. Downplaying his obvious quirks to honor the severity of the situation.

37

"Wow. There are a lot of you. I'm Spencer's dad." Don't know who Spencer is, but I hear a few hushed gasps. "Here's what we know. Spencer broke his nose on the airbag. He fractured a few ribs and has a concussion that they're monitoring, but he's conscious." No one reacts to this news. "Martin," he says, clearing his throat. "Martin's been in surgery since he arrived. We don't know much. His parents ask that you guys keep praying." His facial tension untwists into solemnity, and lets out a giant exhale.

We clap. Not sure why, doesn't seem very appropriate, but the room lights up with thunderous applause. "Fly! Fly! Fly! Fly!" everyone chants.

The all-too familiar rumble of miscalculation disrupts my breathing. What am I doing here? I've included myself in this crowd because Martin and I sat next to each other at graduation. I don't know him beyond some banter and a few hours of sweating together on the football field. If he hadn't spoken to me, I would've read about this on my phone tonight and thought, *Aw, that's sad*, perused his pictures, pretended to know who he was to anyone that asked, and left it at that.

But he did speak to me.

I can barely describe what he looks like. It was too hard for me to look. Tall and wide-grinned is all I've got, with a voice you'd hear above the clatter of any crowded room. But I know how he made me feel. Like it might be worth it to try.

He made me a part of this.

And *this* is much better than solving my own problems.

······

I'm not there anymore. I know that. Wherever I went with Spitty isn't where I am now. What I lived there isn't quite the same as the way *I* remember it happening. And I do remember now. I think?

It's hard to know what is what.

To me, there was a crushing, grinding loudness, then a sudden stop, bringing in its place a ringing hiss everywhere. In my ears. In my chest. My legs. My eyes were open, but in slits, like a wide-screen movie on a thirteen-inch TV or something. Spits was above me. Soaked in blood. He was grabbing me and saying every swear word ever invented. Even some he made up. He was trying to hold something together, and he was shaking badly, like the time the police caught us toilet papering Turrey's house, except this time he was full-on sobbing. More than end of *Rookie of the Year*–level crying. His face looked gnarly. Literally. There was blood pouring out of his nose.

Dripping on me.

On my body.

The body I can't seem to find, because I can't see anything but gray, and I don't know if it's even seeing at all, because I don't think you can see thoughts. They exist on the inside of a blink.

Like me, right now.

······

It's approaching midnight. The crowd has downsized, but you'd never know it by the amount of yellow robes scattered about. Cameron is asleep on Aminah's shoulder with her legs propped on my lap. I'm holding a magazine, using her ankles as an armrest, but really eavesdropping on text-message girl. Her name is Brooke Delgado, and she has identified herself as Martin's girlfriend, which jabs at my heart more than I care to admit. Guess I was right not to give him my number.

Being right is not always satisfying.

Brooke's on the phone with her mom, mixing Spanish and English to relay everything Spencer's dad said earlier. I've been hoping she might have an inside scoop, but it doesn't seem so.

I go to get a Kit Kat from the vending machine, and I overhear that she isn't Martin's girlfriend after all, which bandages up my heart jab far more than it should.

"Stage five clinger," says some kid they call Turrey.

Definitely not meant for my ears. But as a master in the art of multitasking, I can pretend to do up to three different things while listening to someone's conversation. For maximum effect, I bang on the side of the machine to buy myself more time.

"That shit was over months ago. She knows it," Turrey says. "She just wants attention." He catches me looking at him. I dart back to my seat.

"How long do you want to stay?" Aminah asks. She looks like she's over this whole thing, but is willing to provide support for a little longer if need be.

"You guys can go. I think I'm going to stay a little longer."

She shoots me a look. "And how are you planning on getting home?"

"I don't know," I half joke. "But I want a chance to see him."

"Petra Margaret McGowan, be real! This is so weird." She looks *very* over this whole thing now. "What would you tell his parents? Oh yeah, we go way back to five hours ago."

My cheeks burn. "Let's go. I can come back tomorrow."

She makes no effort to hide how much I'm disturbing her, aggressively grabbing my magazine to toss onto a stack. "Daniel wouldn't even come with us here tonight, and he's having a pool day tomorrow, so *he* won't be driving you." She shakes Cameron awake. "You'd have to ask *this* sleeping beauty for a ride. Just taking us here was a big deal, especially since she thought she was leaving her car at your house for the night while we partied our youth away with a bunch of classmates we never met. You know how she gets about wasting gas." Cameron, only half-coherent, gives a thumbs-up to that. "I'm not sure how you plan on doing this again tomorrow."

I don't answer. Just stand up and walk toward the exit. They both follow. No one says goodbye to us. A few odd looks, one quasi grin, but no words.

I'll find a way to get here tomorrow.

5

A yellow sea appears in front of Petra. Students—868, counting herself—cloaked in graduation gowns. She sits among them, smack-dab in the middle. "This again," she mutters in response to the ceremony. She starts chipping off her nail polish to kill the time.

"What?" Martin McGee sits next to her, his fists balled up in anticipation and his eyes wide with terror and fascination.

"I said that, didn't I?" Petra asks him, mortified. But she can't help herself. She keeps talking. "This whole thing is ridiculous. Put on a robe and pretend to care about all of these other people walking across the stage. It doesn't really do justice to what it takes to get to this moment. Although it's kind of perfect, actually. Ninety-five percent wasted time, five percent valuable. Just like high school!" The words pour out, her every passing thought now conversation. "Of course, if I was valedictorian instead of

Steve Taggart, I'm sure I'd be looking out at all these people and thinking the system was perfect."

She stops to consider Martin again. His bewildered stare hasn't changed. If anything, it's grown stronger. "Figures. You're afraid of me because I'm being myself," she says. Her throat goes dry.

"No," Martin says back. There's a fervor to his tone. "Not at all." He shakes off a distracted thought. "I just don't understand what's going on."

"What? With us? Nothing." Her tongue is as sharp as cut glass. She doesn't even want to be harsh with him, but she can't stop. Her usual filter seems to be broken. Her every emotion and thought come out as is, without time to reconsider. Before she can stop herself, she says, "I want to try, but I don't know you well enough to know if it's worth it." This unexpected bout of vulnerability stifles her breath.

The strange mix of confusion and terror on Martin's face grows.

Petra puts her hands over her mouth to prevent herself from saying more.

Hands over mouth.

Not hers anymore. An old memory overtakes the moment, and with a flick, like a remote changing channels, she's in the back of Ryan's Jeep. His callused palm is pressing so hard into her face that her lips fold into her gums.

She's moving. Fighting. Resisting.

Flick.

She's back at graduation, one of 868 again.

The scenery sharpens. Details she hadn't noticed before come into clear view, like the fact that there is a curved wall all around them, and the sky is not a sky, but a ceiling. They're inside a cylinder of sorts. It's dank and gray. And shrinking.

The room is shrinking.

"What just happened?" Martin asks.

Petra doesn't have words. The old memory has affected her like a disease would, preventing her ability to speak.

"Please, just tell me what's going on," Martin pleads.

"Petra Margaret McGowan," a voice calls out from the stage.

Somehow, it's become her time to graduate. She rises as if possessed and scoots down her row out to the center aisle. The other graduates track every step of her silent processional.

Petra picks up her pace, keeping her eyes trained on her feet, hoping to blend in enough that the stares no longer follow her. When she reaches the stage, she begins the walk from left to right, finding a modicum of comfort in this familiar motion. Still she can feel the other graduates' stares growing more critical. She reaches out for a diploma, but there is nothing there.

The other graduates laugh.

Petra can't help herself. She looks out to see their faces.

They don't *have* faces.

Their features are melted into blurs. It should make it easier, but everything becomes more concentrated instead, like the students all have one pair of eyes and one single thought: *Petra is a fraud.*

All the students but one, she realizes.

Martin McGee.

He's sitting still, terrified as ever, desperate for her to acknowledge him.

"Petra," he calls out.

For a moment, the walls aren't shrinking, and the rest of the crowd doesn't matter. There's just Petra and Martin and a question mark between them, begging to be answered.

Petra sprints to the stairs along the other side of the stage, trying to run to Martin. She can see now that he's hurt. Blood glistens on his skin. Glass shards glint.

What happened?

Before she can reach him, the cylinder erases the crowd and closes in on her.

She's trapped.

6

SATURDAY, JUNE 9

Aminah woke me up, texting me at the crack of dawn to ask about swimming today. First of all, school's done. Stop getting up at 6:45 a.m. Second of all, I know I told her less than twelve hours ago that I'd be coming back to the hospital. I can't just forget about what happened to Martin.

With some of the graduation money my grandma sent, the cash my parents said I'm not allowed to touch until I "earn it by getting things sorted out with my academic life," I bribed Jessica to give me a ride to the hospital, which is the only perk of having my sisters in town for the underwhelming almost-culmination of my high school career. It's a true miracle my parents haven't ratted me out to a single person. They're more ashamed of the truth than I am.

Just graduated.

The emergency room people wouldn't give me much information, so my stealth skills got put to good use. I spotted the vending machine guy from yesterday, Turrey, walking in, and I followed him up. Now I'm sitting between him and what appears to be a husband and wife decked out in matching jerseys.

It's a new waiting room. We've been bumped up to the intensive care unit.

The crowd is still impressive in size and just as unfamiliar. Everyone talks or checks their phones. Most do both at once. I don't think anyone knows I'm a part of the Believe Marty Can Fly team. That's the official name. Martin's friend-girl Brooke set up the crowdfunding page about an hour ago, detailing out loud every step along the way. According to her, Martin's entire right side is "destroyed."

When the words pass through her glossed lips, I recoil, like I can actually see how the accident has broken him.

......

I went somewhere else. I had a body I could see and touch, but it was like cardboard or something. I was really stiff, kind of itchy, and wearing my ugly yellow robe. One of 868 again, because it was my graduation, but at the same time, it wasn't *my* graduation, if that makes sense. Which it doesn't.

None of this does.

Petra was there. I really felt something when I saw her, which is a first since I got to wherever I am. For a split second, I had that "Hey! I know you!" sensation you get when you show up to a class you think you have no friends in, only to find someone you're cool with sitting in the front row.

The good feelings went away when I couldn't figure out why we were in some sort of gray tube. Petra didn't seem to find it weird at all, which only made me more concerned. I kept asking her what was going on. She kept getting more upset with me, saying she didn't know me well enough and all this bizarre stuff.

The strangest part of all was that, for a split second, the graduation place disappeared altogether, and I came back here, to the blink. Before I could process it, I flickered back to the graduation place again.

It was wild.

When I returned, Petra was withdrawn, like something really horrible had happened to her in that lost flicker of time. She wouldn't speak to me at all. Out of nowhere, the announcer guy called for her to graduate. She started walking, and the entire crowd stared at her like she was a Cardinals fan at a Cubs game or something. She got to the stage, and she looked right at me. For a moment, we were just watching each other. An unexpected sadness built up in my throat. All the weird, unexplainable stuff didn't matter. I just wanted to be someone she could trust. I didn't want these other people to keep staring at her like she was broken. I wanted to fix it all, make it better, but I couldn't. I was useless. I called her name, and she tried to run to me, but the gray tube somehow closed her in, and I came back to here.

It wasn't my place to help. It just wasn't my place in general.

But there I was.

And here I am.

......

"Are you okay?" the young woman next to me asks after I finish chipping off what little remains of my nail polish.

"What?" I say, not sure if she means me.

She switches her tactic. "Do you know Marty?"

"Oh." I contemplate being honest but decide excessive exposition would confuse her. "Yeah." Not an untruth.

"I'm his sister, Katie. This is my husband, Rick."

I give them both somber handshakes. "Petra."

"That's a cool name," Katie says.

"I like it enough." I can tell by her expression that I sound cold. I don't mean to. Conversational walls tend to pop up when I'm uncomfortable. "It's a family name."

"It's nice. Thanks for coming out to support Marty."

Maybe it's inappropriate of me, but I take the opportunity to get some more information. "Of course. How is he?"

Katie leans in. "I saw him this morning. His face—" She starts to tear up, and I know I've crossed some kind of line, because her eyes soften, disregarding my coldness and accepting me as an outsider in which she can confide. She must need an outlet. "It's not our Marty."

I nod like I know. I kind of do?

"I couldn't take it. I'm better sitting out here. My mom and dad are camped out in his room until the next surgery. I'm sure you know my mom. Or Mama Dorothy, as she prefers," Katie says with the ghost of a laugh.

I start to come clean, my mouth forming an *um*. I feel incapable of continuing my undeserved role as friend with privileged knowledge, but Katie's face lights up, thinking I'm making a confirming gesture. "God, everyone knows my mom. She's wearing Marty's old football jersey. He played two JV games his freshman year before he quit, but Mom's all *It shows what a fighter he is.*"

"She's right," I note back. It's what has to be said.

Staring at Katie, taking in her wide eyes and full mouth, spread from smiling over her mother's apparent ridiculousness, I try to conjure up a picture of Mama Dorothy. Martin mentioned her at graduation, and both kids called her by that name. She must be the type of mom who goes overtime on the job, chaperoning all field trips, showing up to sporting events that don't even involve her kids, shepherding the masses with her aggressive enthusiasm and charm. Short and hovering around her late forties, sensible haircut with some blond highlights to disguise impending gray, and the kind of smile that could turn up to ten or cut you down to size depending on her mood.

"They don't know how many more surgeries he'll need. Or when he'll wake up. They keep saying, 'He's not out of the woods yet.' If you're gonna try to see him, go now," Katie says, on the verge of tears. "You'd be braver than me."

My guilty eyes don't even have time to meet her gaze before her phone starts ringing.

"Hold on," she says. She answers the call, and I divert my

attention to my lap, listening in. It's an aunt. Katie gives her the rundown, choking out details as her husband pats her back.

Turrey's been eyeballing me this entire time, giving off a silent judgment that expects a "What?" or "Hi" or "You're right—I should leave" from me.

I've trapped myself. The only way out is to see Martin.

Well, maybe not the only way, but it's the way I choose.

What can I say? I'm pretty great at making questionable choices.

......

Wait. I get it now. It's so obvious. Don't know why it didn't come to me sooner. *This is all a dream.* Graduation is tomorrow, and I'm doing a weird subconscious *Inception*-style life lesson thing.

Man, did I eat before bed? This is like when Turrey did wrestling, and he wasn't eating so he could make weight. He started having hallucinations in the middle of health class. Mr. Hubert and I had to drag him to the nurse's office.

I made up an actual hours-long graduation ceremony, then topped it off with some over-the-top car accident with Spits. Probably represents my fear of what the future will bring us or something. That's what Katie will say when I tell her about this. She loves dream analysis. She'll tell me I'm living inside Spitty's perspective because I care about how he views the world or something. Then she'll say I made up Petra because she represents everything I wish I could have, and the weird thing with her inside the gray tube has something to do with my fears of messing up good things that happen to me.

51

You know what? I don't even need to ask Katie. I've got it all down myself.

······

I'm up and moving, headed out of the waiting room and around the corner, where the words *Intensive Care Unit* run across the middle of two doors. A buzzer is on the left wall. If I press it, I am Alice, and this is the rabbit hole. I've hovered around the edge, definitely dangled a leg over, but I haven't fallen in yet.

I press the button.

"Hello," says a fuzzy voice.

"Hi, I'm here to see Martin McFly...I mean, McGee."

Bzzzt. The door opens.

Down I fall.

The nurse who buzzed me in sits behind a counter. "He's straight ahead," she says.

The walls are beige, not white. The rooms are quiet, not buzzing with doctors screaming indecipherable jargon over one another while defibrillating chests and stitching up gaping wounds. It's not at all the picture hammered into my brain by TV shows and movies. Maybe that's what the emergency room is supposed to look like? I'm lucky enough to never have had to know for sure. The ICU exists on its own wavelength altogether. There's a vague sense of doom permeating the hallways, masked by clean scents and good ventilation.

Martin's name is posted next to an open door. His parents stand against the inside wall of his room, neglecting chairs that surround a not-yet-visible bed. Bouquets are everywhere space allows.

Tragedy makes people so efficient.

Mama Dorothy is more than I expected. She swims in Martin's football jersey, shorter and stouter than I calculated. I can smell baked goods and cigarettes on her. His dad's not the Jim Carrey via *The Majestic* I had predicted though. Not an ounce. He's very tall and very thin, as if his entire existence is extremities. Very pointed noise. Very sharp jaw. Very kind eyes.

I tiptoe in, my heart beating up into my throat. Mama Dorothy takes one look and pulls me to her chest, not a word of introduction spoken between us. She rubs my back in soothing circles, her head nestled into my shoulder. "I'm sorry, Mrs. McGee," I whisper.

She jerks me away from her. "Please. It's Mama Dorothy."

I fumble over my words for an apology. She tidies my ponytail and kisses my forehead. I can't tell if she's mistaken me for someone else or if this is just her being her. I look to Mr. McGee, and he offers a vague, "Nice to see you."

I turn to Martin.

It's a lot to take in. He's half a person. Literally. The right side of his face is so swollen that it looks fake. I gasp and well up, taken by the gravity of the matter.

This looks like television. A daytime soap opera in dimmer lighting.

But it's real, I remind myself. And familiar, somehow. His battered self makes me think of the dream I had last night. I was at graduation. And he was there, covered in blood and shards of glass.

I shake my head in disbelief.

Nausea hits, a by-product of my speedy and dizzying descent into the life and near-death of Martin McGee.

......

Something is off about this dream though. I thought you couldn't actually, *you know* in one. That's what Katie always says. I guess I didn't really, *you know* earlier. I was in the process of *you know*-ing.

Don't want to think it because I'm afraid it's a jinx, but I mean being, uh, not quite alive.

......

We stand in silence, looking at Martin. On his good side, I notice his eyelashes are quite long. They rest along his upper cheekbone, fanning out from corner to corner. His eyeballs move beneath the lids. My pulse jumps, and so do I, automatically, like a grasshopper avoiding a footstep. If Martin wakes up, I will be the first person he sees.

Mama Dorothy lets out a sharp *ha*, not meant to be mean but definitely laced with something bitter. "They say it's normal," she tells me. "I'll take it. Means my Marty's still fighting in there."

A strange, piercing ache pings in my chest. A part of me, selfishly, unfairly, wanted to be the first face he sees. Maybe to prove to myself that this is exactly where I'm supposed to be. My personal stuff can wait. What's one more day?

I pinch my arm. I'm thinking this while looking at someone who might die. *Die*. One more day is a lot.

All throughout graduation, I tried not to let myself glimpse more than his profile. I figured if I knew what he looked like, then everything I had started to feel between us would be real. And I couldn't do real.

Now, I notice a fresh tan line cutting his neck in half. Must be from the dress shirt under his gown. Little craters of scalp are showing from where a razor pulled in too tight on the sides of his head. It will all even out in a week's time because he's a boy, and they are lucky like that. They never seem to wear mistakes for long.

This is so intimate. A privilege not ever granted to near strangers, watching someone sleep, studying the intricate details of their being. I can't help but fixate on a faint scar above his upper lip. Mama Dorothy and Mr. McGee stay perched along the wall like they don't want to get too close, but they can't bear to be too far.

Why am I not afraid to be so close? It's not right. Or normal. It's driving extra slow past an accident to gather up as many details as I can. I force myself to turn away. The second my body pivots, Mama Dorothy wraps her arms around me once again.

"What's happening?" I ask, a question more for myself than her.

"Nothing we can't handle," Mama Dorothy says.

This is too much. I wiggle out and walk away, trying not to look back but unable to stop myself. The McGees wave. The nurse does too.

They don't even know my name.

......

In my heart I know that when it happens to me for real, I'll be a one-hundred-year-old dude, sitting on my front porch kicking back a fine bottle of whiskey and telling stories to my great-grandkids. I'll finish up the one about how I charmed Grandma. They will all know the tale by heart, but they will listen like it's the first time they've ever heard it. I will tell it like it's the first time I've ever lived it. It will choke me up, and I will excuse myself to go upstairs. I'll fall asleep holding a picture of her, never to wake up again.

Mina Lonigan and Brooke Delgado. Those are the only girls I've ever dated, which is not too bad for an eighteen-year-old. But neither one of them was close to being my lucky lady for life. I'm looking forward to that. Finding a girl who likes talking to me when I don't feel like being Fly. Who tolerates sports enough to go to games with Katie, her husband, and me. Who keeps my bullshit in check but doesn't mind when I air-guitar the classics in the middle of a grocery store.

A girl who calls me Martin.

Somewhere way down the line, like in my late twenties or something, I plan on getting my life together.

For now, I need to wake up.

......

I get as far as the elevator before I collapse, tucking my body into a corner. The wall hugs my right side and a gigantic potted plant holds my left. Without these surfaces, I'd surely combust. My body would crack open and let all the strange things inside of me spill out onto this shiny linoleum floor.

My phone, long neglected in my pocket, vibrates. I pull it out to see eight missed calls and six voicemails from my parents. It's clear Jessica did not tell them where she'd taken me. Nice.

My eyes skim for any interesting texts and land upon Mr. Valedictorian himself, Steve Taggart.

> Word on the street is that I won't be seeing you at Notre Dame after all. Is it true? You always did have a hard time with math. I have some packets from middle school if you need them.

Of course he'd find out. If anyone cares more than my parents about my rapid descent in class rank, it's Steve. I couldn't be in less of a mood for his backward flirtation, and I don't want to even go near the parental drama I've stirred up. I close out of my texts and open Instagram to type in Martin McGee. How unfair to meet his face in its damaged state. While I'm safe in my corner, I have to know who he used to be. The small little circle of a photo meant to represent him is a picture of young Michael J. Fox. His most recent picture is a body shot of him standing on what looks to be a beer pong table, cape around his neck, hands stretched to the side as if he's flying. The time stamp tells me it's over three years old. I pinch the screen to zoom in on his face. It's pixelated, but I see Mama Dorothy in his grin. The rest of his account pictures are of Cubs players or different pairs of sneakers.

I scroll through his tagged photos. Not one of them ever gets close to his face. He's always turned away from the camera. Turrey, from the vending machine yesterday and the waiting room today, is in almost all of them. It makes sense why he stared me down. He is a member of the innermost circle of Martin's social group, one that probably has the rings of an ancient tree, and he knows I come from a different world altogether.

"Hey," a voice calls out to me. "Who are you?"

Like the universe heard my thoughts and brought him to me, it's Turrey. He walks up to my potted plant corner, investigating my suspicious nature without hesitation. He picks up the plant and scoots it over so he has room to sit beside me.

"I'm Petra," I tentatively answer, as if that may or may not be who I am.

"You know Fly?"

I decide to be honest. "Kind of. He sat next to me at graduation."

"And you're here?"

He's so to the point with all of his statements that I get that helpless feeling that comes along every so often, like when I've misplaced an assignment or slept through an alarm. "I just feel really bad about what happened."

"I'm Mike."

"I thought your name was Turrey."

"Are you some kind of stalker? That's my last name."

"Oh," I say, shrinking by the second. Turrey's fast-talking, quick-thinking, ball-busting confidence gives me whiplash. It makes me too confused to break open, which is the only plus side.

"I've seen you before," he says.

"Hm," I answer, not sure where this is going. "I don't think I know you."

"That's cool…" He drifts off, his interest directed more toward the plant than me. "Wanna get out of here? Fly's got another surgery in half an hour. We'll come back after."

If there is a course correction to be made, a way to stop myself from dropping farther down the rabbit hole, I can't see it. So while falling, I might as well fall spectacularly.

"Sure," I say.

7

I'm pretty done with this dream, and the somewhere, every-where, nowhere place I am. It's making me think of the time Mama Dorothy hauled me to the mall super early to hunt for Black Friday deals. I got separated from her, and a bunch of competi-tive adults swept me up in their pack. They figured I belonged to another woman among them. Thought my crying had to do with the usual little boy problems. Boredom. Hunger. Tiredness. Lack of toys. At some point, I started holding my breath, sick of that weird Williams-Sonoma smell all older ladies at the mall carry with them. About to pass out, I swayed into this blond woman with bug eyes and lipstick on her teeth. She looked at me and said, "Little one, who is your mommy?"

I got returned to Mama D, and after she chewed out every person who would listen, and some who wouldn't, we went home. We had to take the bus because I wouldn't unwrap my arms from around her hips. "If anything ever happens to you again," she said, "don't worry. I'll always find you. I'll handle it."

It's like I'm there again, stuck in the middle of a tornado with no one bothering to notice yet. I'd really like for my mom to walk into my bedroom right now and shake me awake. You know, find me and handle it.

......

When in doubt, mall it out. Even I live by this rule. It's the universal, uniting space for all social groups. Turrey—I feel oddly more comfortable calling him that than Mike—drives us here without asking. The wheels of his truck are hiked up so high it's like cliff diving to reach land, so he walks around to my side and extends his hand out to help me down. Neglecting his gesture, I leap.

Catapulted forward, I'm instead hurtling myself out of Ryan's Jeep, the air acting as a temporary harness, holding me up as words twist around, taking cruel shapes in my mind. The pavement stings my shins on impact, releasing me to the present.

I'm here.

It's just a memory.

I'm here.

"Okay?" Turrey asks.

My hands are sweaty, and I'm digging my fingernails into my palms, standing idly outside of Turrey's gigantic truck. Not Ryan's Jeep. "I just like to do it myself."

Turrey shakes his head and starts walking toward the entrance. I don't bother keeping pace because he's not much for small talk, which I appreciate, especially now, rattled by the aftershocks of what just worked its way to the surface.

Turrey heads to the food court, and our respectful silence is broken only by the word, "Pizza?" To which I nod. As we wait in line, I text Cameron.

Today's even weirder than yesterday

       What?
       Why?
       Did you go back to the hospital?

Yeah
I saw him

       WHAT?!

Yeah. His sister told me to go see him
So I did
It was so weird
I don't know why I did it

       OMG Petra
       What'd he look like

A mummy basically
But he's alive

Just unconscious

He has another surgery today

> Omg
>
> What are you doing now
>
> We're swimming at Daniels!
>
> You should come!
>
> I want to hear more about this

I can't

I'm at the mall with Mike Turrey

> I'm sorry. Who?!??

I'll explain later

We get our pizza and find a table. Turrey smothers his slice of sausage with unfathomable amounts of cheese. "Need some?" he asks. He hands it to me. It's not a question. I give the shaker a few smacks over my cheese and set it down. "So?" he says as a precursor to his first bite. "What's your deal?"

"My deal?" Our car ride broke some barriers. He's a little less intimidating now that we've both hummed along to Top 40 radio together.

"Exactly," he responds, like, *Figure it out on your own. I'm not getting more specific.*

I mimic his confidence. It always helps to pretend. "You first."

"Played a lot of sports, but just basketball and football this year. Going to ISU."

"Okay. I ranked eleventh in the class. Did a lot of activities. No sports. Going to Notre Dame." My default answer spills out of my mouth before I remember that it's not the way I want to define myself. And that it's not exactly true, anyways.

Turrey laughs at me the way most people do. Intimidated, impressed, and somewhat embarrassed. For themselves or for me, I've never been able to determine.

Suddenly I want to let out a little of my mess. "Actually, I might not be able to go," I say.

"What do you mean?"

"I didn't technically graduate."

He coughs on his straw. "What?"

"Yeah."

Turrey looks away from his pizza to recalibrate his image of me. "I thought you were Miss Eleventh in the Class?"

Just graduated. "I am." He looks confused. "It's complicated. I missed my Honors Algebra II final last year. Instead of failing me, Ms. Hornsby gave me an incomplete, so my GPA got weighed differently than it would've if I'd gotten a letter grade. It's kind of confusing, but basically she helped me out."

"Damn. Hornsby straight up stole my phone for a week when she caught me texting during an assembly." He shakes his head. "How'd you get her to do that?"

His reaction is unexpectedly understated. I exhale a bit. "Well, before I was Miss Eleventh, I was Miss Second. I'm not great at math, but I always tried really hard, and I did all of Ms. Hornsby's ridiculous extra credit assignments, which she liked. No one does those. She told me I could retake the exam at the beginning of this year or repeat the class. I didn't do either. Then she said I could take the test during winter finals. I didn't. Without the credit, my rank fell. Now the administration's agreed to let it be a pass or fail mark instead of a letter grade, so I meet the minimum course requirements to graduate."

"That sure is a lot of strings getting pulled on your behalf. You realize that, right?"

"Yeah. I do." My heavy tongue chokes my words until they're nothing but dead syllables. "Juniors take the final on Monday. That's my last chance."

"You going?"

It's a complicated question, and there are too many ways to answer, so I do what I always do: keep quiet.

Turrey's face contorts into an expression resembling a crinkled paper bag. "Whatever happened, you can't fix it by ignoring it. They're giving you a chance people like me don't get. You understand? You need to take it."

I nod. I do understand.

To change the subject, I go in big. "So, how do you know Martin?"

Turrey laughs. "Haven't heard anyone other than a teacher call him that in, like, ten years. Fly's my oldest friend. You know Spits?"

I shake my head.

"He was driving."

"Oh."

Turrey devours the rest of his slice then dabs at the corners of his mouth. "It's weird as hell that you came, but Fly'd like knowing some random smart girl rolled up to check on him," he says.

"I'm glad."

"Fly's pretty smart too. He doesn't think we know, but his mom's always bragging."

"Where's he going to school?"

"He's taking a year off to save up for ISU with me and Spitty. Brooke's trying to get money for the hospital stuff through some crowdfunding page she made."

He brought her up first, so I crack the small window of opportunity open. "Brooke's his girlfriend, right?"

Turrey belly laughs. He sips on his Mountain Dew. "They mess around."

I offer him a polite nod and pick up the last bite of my pizza, wondering what Ryan told his high school friends about me last year. If I come up in conversation with his new college friends or if he erased me from his history like I've done to him. A life chapter never spoken aloud by either side.

"Why? You wanna date Fly?" Turrey asks.

The question sets my face on fire. I just know Turrey's the type to comment on the way I'm blushing, so I bite down on my tongue to stop myself from feeling anything other than a burst of pain. "I barely know him," I say to diffuse.

He throws his head back in hysterics, clutching at the air to hold on to the laughter seizing him. "Says the girl who's missing finals and shit to come to the hospital."

"It's on Monday," I protest.

"Yeah, all right, whatever, I'm not gonna get in your business. But I tell you what—Fly would go for it, one hundred percent."

I mumble about how I heard him call Brooke a stage-five clinger. I try to stop myself from saying it, but not so hard that I actually do.

"For real, do you have a wire on me? It's like this: Brooke and Fly have love, but it's not *love*. It's over, but she's acting like it isn't because of what happened." He lets out a healthy yawn, one so big that I yawn too.

The Brooke topic dies within our long stretches of air intake. I'll have to get more information elsewhere.

"I didn't sleep last night," he starts. "Nobody did. We all stayed up just kind of staring at the hospital walls."

"I bet," I say. I wish insomnia would find me. There are certain recurring themes my mind forces me to visit every time I close my eyes. It's, like, I get it. I deal with it enough while I'm awake.

Turrey inhales and pauses, the first sign of hesitation I've seen from him since we met. I stop chewing just so I can take it in. "I could right now."

It's not a question, but he means it as one. "Do you want to sleep in your truck?" I ask, not sure if I've read him right. It seems so random.

"I don't think I can drive if I don't."

"Oh." A little smile creeps up on me, happy to know that I read him perfectly. It flattens out when I mull over his words again. "Oh." What's one more reluctant yes in the bigger picture? After what happened to Martin, any mention of unsafe driving is a good enough reason to do something, no matter how strange. "That's fine."

"Damn food always makes me tired," Turrey curses as he throws his garbage away.

Maybe I'll study while he sleeps.

Maybe.

What a word.

8

In the center of a hazy version of Turrey's bedroom sits a makeshift poker table. The space is all dim corners and lazily maintained pieces of decor. Clouds of smoke fog the room. It smells like stale air conditioning. It feels like the stillness inside an idle car.

Before Mike Turrey takes his seat, he puts on opaque sunglasses to cover the truth his eyes will surely show. One by one, the other players appear. Spencer Kuspits sits on Turrey's left, smiling because he should. Because he can. Because it's all he knows how to do. Chris Davis is on his right, typically smug. And Petra McGowan presides over them all, dealing the cards with the precision of a time-tested expert.

The boys are dressed in tuxedos—the same ones they wore to prom, sans top hats and canes. Spencer is in white and pink. Chris is in black and gold. Turrey is the sleekest in a rich dark brown, almost as dark as his skin, accented with a black tie.

Petra wears jean shorts and a heather-gray crewneck tee. *That's not right,* Turrey thinks. In a flash, Petra's dressed in a white button down with a black vest over it, her hair slicked back into a neat low ponytail.

No words are spoken or looks shared. It's all steely stares and quiet grimaces. The stakes are too high. A life is on the line. The life of Martin McGee.

Martin, a.k.a Fly himself, is off to the side, elevated on a pedestal constructed from old beer cans, wearing the custom Cubs jersey Turrey got him for his sixteenth birthday. The players know of Fly's presence, but no one reacts when he yells out, "Hello? Hello? Why won't anyone look at me!" They don't even glance in his direction. He is nothing more than a physical representation of why they are playing.

Petra silently deals five cards to every player. When Turrey turns his hand over to look, each card is not a number, but a good memory with Fly. He understands the rules of the game: choose which card you think is the best memory and place it down in front of you. Once everyone's chosen, the group has to vote for which card wins the round. When a winner is decided, all other entries from that round are thrown out, the memories erased from existence. Replace your discard with another card from the deck until the pile runs out. The player with the most winning memories gets the right to be the most upset about what's happened to Fly.

The first card Turrey looks at is the time in fifth grade when Fly decided he was going to climb the flagpole. For Turrey's eyes and ears only, the card starts playing out the action of the day like a movie.

A young Martin hypes himself up, clapping his hands together and dropping down to do push-ups, putting on a big show. It's fall. The bite in the air has painted red splotches onto his cheeks, only further exaggerated by the effort he's putting into preparing.

A small crowd of fifth graders gathers around him. Young Turrey, Spits, and Chris stand together at the front, never more than a step or two away from one another. Young Spits's teeth push out over his lower lip as he stands gawking. Young Chris shifts from foot to foot, rubbing his arms furiously to fight the cold. He's forgotten his jacket once again. Young Turrey is jumping in place, excited for what's to come. He starts yelling words of encouragement to both Martin and the crowd. "Let's go!" and "Come on now!" He's met with small cheers every time.

Martin announces he's ready. He takes a step back then leaps to the pole, wrapping himself around it like a koala. He starts scooting up, his face tense with concentration. Around the ninth scoot, he loses his energy and slides down so fast the crowd gasps.

"Ow!" he yells out, more theatrical than genuine. He leaps back up. "Let's try that again."

Young Turrey turns to the crowd, cupping his hand behind his ear to make the other kids cheer louder. This goes on a few more times, each of Martin's attempts to climb more pathetic than the last. However, the crowd turns more and more hysterical, growing in size and volume, lathered up into a true frenzy.

"Fly! Fly! Fly!" the fifth graders chant at Turrey's beckoning. A new nickname is born right on the spot.

Principal Wheeler catches on and runs over to the flagpole. She presses her hand into Martin's back and directs him toward her office, the entire crowd chanting his new name as they walk away.

Turrey doesn't even have to examine the other cards in his hand. This card is the moment Martin McGee learned how to entertain a crowd. This card is the moment Martin McGee became Fly.

This card can't be beat.

Turrey places it on the table, smiling as he does it. So much for poker faces.

Once all the cards have been laid down, one by one the memories are projected onto the blank wall above Turrey's bed. Spits and Chris laugh hysterically at Spits's card. It shows the time Fly dressed in a full wet suit to ask Brooke to prom. Fly gathers up all the other dancers on Brooke's Poms team. They put on shark fins and do a hastily choreographed number to LL Cool J's song "Deepest Bluest" from the movie *Deep Blue Sea*. Fly performs the song with modified lyrics, somehow making it about the dance.

It's funny, but it's not Fly's best work.

The memory ends. Without deliberation, the others vote for it. Spits even votes for himself. Turrey forgets to vote, that's how flustered he is. The boys don't notice. They see a majority in favor and call it a win. The rejected cards dissolve into the poker table, memories erased.

"Wait! Absolutely not," Fly calls out from his beer can perch. At this, Turrey can't help but turn to look at him, surprised at his outburst. "Turrey's card was obviously the best. That was one of the greatest days of my whole life! It can't just be gone. I mean, I did crush that lyrical rewrite, but absolutely not. Plus, Turrey was the one who gave me the ice pack from his lunch box because I bruised my tailbone so badly that day at the flagpole. He deserves to win."

Turrey stands up. He walks over to Fly's perch and hugs Fly close. "I know I don't really do this kind of shit, but I love you, man," he says, tears in his eyes. "Please come back to us."

9

It happened again.

I was with Turrey, Spits, and Chris. Petra was there too. They weren't paying attention to me even though they were all gambling for…me? I kept asking what was going on, but no one would even look at me. I was up on this beer can throne in my Cubs jersey, watching over them.

Their cards played memories from my life. Seeing myself in different stages—smiling and laughing and being the general jackass I've grown to be—made my heart numb out and my knees cave in. The only thing I knew for sure was that after they picked a winner from the round, all the other memories were supposed to disappear forever.

They picked me in a wet suit sweating my ass off dancing with Brooke's Poms team, trying to get her to go to prom with me. It was a good memory for sure, but it wasn't the one that should last. How could I be reduced to just that day?

Turrey's been there for me since we were playing Pee Wee together in kindergarten. That kid was the first person to ever invite me to play sports during recess. He was dribbling a ball, getting ready to start up a round of foursquare, and he yelled out, "Hey, Martin! We need one more. You in?" Freakin' six years old, and he could see I needed a friend.

I had to speak up and defend the card he chose. I didn't care if they weren't going to listen. After I finished talking, Turrey told me he loved me and that he needed me to come back to them. As much as I've been through with that kid, it's always been out of love. We both know that, but it gets me to hear him say it, especially when I don't know why he felt it needed to be spoken. Or why he was so upset. Or what he meant by *Please come back to us*.

Like wake up?

Believe me, Turrey, I'm trying.

......

Turrey's slumped over the steering wheel, snoring. He really did need it. I don't think I've ever seen a person fall asleep so effortlessly. We're in the back of the mall lot, where no cars dare park unless it's the day after Thanksgiving or the day before Christmas. Turrey left the engine running so the air could stay on, but I open my window anyway. I stretch my hand out, and my fingers pinch distant trees that stand as islands in the concrete ocean around us.

Without warning, Turrey wakes up, as abrupt and effortless as his descent into sleep.

"Welcome back," I say.

"I had a weird dream."

"Just now?"

"Yeah. I saw Fly."

"That's nice."

"Yeah." He turns up the radio to hum along.

There's no way I'm going home now. "Could you drop me off at my friends?" I ask. I give him Daniel's address so he can plug it into his GPS.

"That's my address," he says back.

A misplaced two instead of a four, and I stumble on the discovery that Mike Turrey and Daniel Stetson are neighbors. I realize I've seen Turrey before—granted, through a fence or from a second-floor balcony—but I have years' worth of squinted glances into his home life. His family loves to throw huge backyard parties. We even snuck into one. His little brother and sister publicly hate each other, staging outdoor fights with the regularity of a scripted reality show, always finding new ways to scream children's versions of obscenities at each other. When they think no one is watching, they get along perfectly.

"I knew I'd seen you before," Turrey says. "You're at Daniel's a lot."

"Yeah. He's one of my best friends."

"Cool," Turrey answers, his favorite drifting response. He starts up the engine and rolls the windows down lower.

I stretch my hand out to feel the warm air blow through my fingers.

I went to the same school as Martin. The same mall. I've had the same skeleton of a life. Now I know his family. I know one of his best friends. How interesting to paint a picture of someone when they aren't around to help with the shading.

What picture does the world paint of me? I wonder. *And how close is it to the truth?*

Not very, I answer as I pretend to smash a distant oak tree between my thumb and my index finger.

I don't know Martin at all.

But I feel like I do.

I feel like I do.

10

urrey parks in his winding driveway and walks me over to Daniel's. He follows me as I open the back gate, walk through the vegetable garden, and end up at the edge of the in-ground pool. Apparently, Turrey is coming with me.

"Petra!" Cameron shouts, emerging from her shaded corner to greet me. She sees Turrey and tries to communicate in glances, asking *Why is he here?* with only her eyes. She's so distracted by his presence that she hugs me while dripping wet. Her one-piece soaks the front of my shirt.

"This is Mike Turrey," I tell her. "Turns out he lives next door."

They shake hands. It's all so forced. I wander off to put my purse down on a pool chair.

Aminah emerges from the guesthouse. "Hello," she says more to Turrey than me, sizing him up as a candidate for her affections.

Her gold bikini shimmers in the sun, popping against the umber of her skin.

"Sup," Turrey responds.

Aminah dives headfirst into the pool and glides through the water. She surfaces on the other side and holds on to the pool's edge, keeping her back turned to us. Knowing she has no plans to engage in the conversation further—aggressive disinterest a time-tested Aminah Prabhu dating ritual—I ask Cameron, "Where's Daniel?"

"Oh, he's inside," she tells me. Her eyes shift as she sways.

For a girl with a cherub's face and a near-impeccable GPA, Cameron's had a tiny share of debauchery, once dancing in her underwear by Daniel's pool, a beer can in either hand, singing *America the Beautiful*. She's selective in her moments, but when she lets loose, she means it. She hovers around the buzzed stage right now, reaching her hands out for objects that aren't there in an attempt to steady herself.

The worst thing that can happen to a person in a social setting is happening to Turrey, and he doesn't even realize. He's the elephant in the room. His existence is the question, the point of awkwardness, the nervous fidget. Cameron wants to hear about Martin, but she can't ask because Turrey's here, and she doesn't know enough about him to take a chance. Aminah continues dismissing him, alternating between underwater laps and inflatable lounging. The kitchen curtains flutter where Daniel spies on us from inside the house. Turrey doesn't budge.

The intense daylight begs for me to take a break. I sit and apply lotion, attempting to sunbathe in jean shorts and a wet crewneck tee. It isn't easy, but it's much better than trying to keep a conversation going between Turrey and my friends.

Heat beats down on the lounge chair. Sweat pools on the back of my neck where my hair sits crumpled against the wicker chaise. My eyes are closed, but the sun burns red through the lids, lighting up my thoughts, which are full of equations. Letters and numbers converging in a way that requires more of my focus than I'm willing to give. My mind zooms out and sees the paper the equations are written on: a single sheet on a thick stack sitting on the desk in my bedroom. The letters actually scream, as if they aren't letters but people, crying out in neglect. They move around. Questions asking other questions. *If X equals Y, then why aren't you here to study? Can you track the vertical shift of what you're doing to your future? $P(E$ or $T)R^a = S(T/U) P+(I-D)$.*

I tuck the problems away into my overcrowded attic of a mind. Soon. I will study soon. All I need to do is pass. And if I don't, I lose the precious scholarship money my parents mention any chance they get.

Petra, you can't just throw away tens of thousands of dollars because you're upset about a breakup!

My thoughts move to the reddish-blackness I see with closed eyes.

What does Martin see behind his?

I go back to his fanned-out eyelashes. His trimmed hair. That scar on his lip. His Facebook page. Van Halen.

......

I spend my time focusing on my thoughts. It makes more sense to still use those words—*time* and *thoughts*—even though the nothingness seems to swallow everything up.

I need to be the Martin who gave an impromptu knock-'em-dead speech at his sister's wedding, not the Martin who slept through a whole lecture in U.S. History then drew pictures on the pop quiz that followed.

Starting with Petra seems like my best bet. She's the one thought I had while I was in the car with Spitty. I even imagined her at that card game with Turrey.

She's been my constant.

I focus on her name. Petra Margaret McGowan. *Petty Margs.* I try to see her better. I don't have much to go on. Red cheeks and chipped sparkle nails. The light around her when the sun hit her face. Her long brown hair flowing over the back of the folding chair. Van Halen.

11

Petra tries to jump into a pool, hoping to be relieved of the relentless heat. The water is crystal blue and full of people. But Petra doesn't go under. The liquid hardens where her feet touch. It scorches like pavement. She hopscotches, trying not to burn her soles, dodging heads and complaints simultaneously.

"Look out!" someone yells.

"Stay out of my way!" says another.

She does her best, bouncing around as many people as she can. A few heads go under as she catches them with her gazelle glide. Some people grab at her ankles out of spite. Most scream obscenities at her.

She is ruining the party.

The edge of the pool gets farther away with every hop she makes toward it. She stops, stranded in an impossible middle. Her feet burn. The pain is immense, but to her, it's better than being chastised. There's no room in her mind to hide the hurtful words. Make them not matter. She begins to cry, unable to find a solution.

"Petra!" a voice calls out.

She scans for the source, examining the faces of countless strangers half-submerged in a pool she identifies as Daniel's, though most aspects are different. It's an *idea* of Daniel's pool, more of a feeling than an actual thing.

"Please," the voice says. "Over here."

She finds the source.

Martin.

Some features are correct. His height, as it would be in four feet of water. The neat line of a fresh haircut traced into his sunburned neck. His long eyelashes. Everything else Petra pulls from other places. A face that can't seem to be ignored these days, some Ryan Hales pops up in Martin's jaw and eyebrows. Cameron's freckles. The lips of an actor she saw in a commercial playing on repeat in the hospital. All of it pasted together to complete her version of Martin.

She sprints over, ignoring the complaints and slaps along the way. When she reaches him, she kneels. Her feet are damaged beyond repair, and her shins and knees begin to burn, too, flesh crackling under the invisible flames.

"I'm stuck," Martin says.

"So am I," she answers, using a voice so small it barely registers. Pain is diminishing her ability to speak.

"No. I'm *stuck*."

She leans back, puzzled.

"I can't wake up," he adds.

The burning intensifies. Petra fights to find the words she needs. "Of course not," she says. "You're in my dream."

Martin leans back as if he's lost his balance.

Staying in one place for this long has made the pain unbearable. Petra grabs at her throat, finding emptiness where sound should come out. She's wants to say more, but she can't. Everything hurts too much.

Martin tries to reach for her. His hand gets so close. An inch away. "I'm all right," she mumbles, seeing his outstretched fingers through the slits in her own. "You're the one everyone should be worried about."

"What do you mean?"

"Your accident," she whispers.

"Petra!" she hears from someplace outside this pool. "Wake up!"

She begins to shake.

12

P etra! Wake up! I need you to…help me put on some aloe in the bathroom," Cameron says, shaking me. Her figure blocks out the sun. She tugs at my arm until I stand to shake off my drowsiness.

I must've dozed off.

"Oh," I say in reaction to Turrey lying on his stomach next to me. His shirt is now a pillow, leaving his back fully exposed.

"Yeah," Cameron answers.

"Where is everybody?"

"Putting on aloe. Come on."

I follow her into the guesthouse, and she drags me into the bathroom. It's Cameron, Aminah, Daniel, me, a toilet, a sink, and not an inch to spare.

"What's going on?" Aminah whispers.

"What do you mean?"

"What is Michael Turrey doing here?" Daniel snips, a quick scissor cut into our conversation.

"He drove me home. He's your neighbor."

"I'm very aware."

"Do you hate him?"

"No," Daniel snips again.

"What did I do?"

Aminah pinches me. "You're losing your mind!" she says. "I ask again. What is going on with you?"

"Nothing!" I shout.

Aminah glares at me. "You've been weird all week. Maybe all year, if I'm being honest. This is so not nothing!"

I hope for Cameron to be on my side, to take Aminah up on the fight she's angling for—I'm never the source of these things; I never get involved—but right now she's a silent fourth wheel, smashed into the door. She is applying aloe. At least that's true.

"You don't know Martin," Daniel says. His snips are getting bigger. The scissor is dangerously close to making a real cut.

"So what? Why can't I be supportive?"

"You visited him in the hospital! People are still saying he could die, wishing they could see him again, and you actually did it. You took away time that someone who knows him could've used!" The words sting. Even more when it registers that they came from Cameron, who never involves me. Who never makes me the source of these things.

I look up, finding all their eyes coating me with guilt.

......

It's not my dream.

I'm trying to let that sink in and become something I can actually believe. For some reason, it still makes more sense that I'm the one that's dreaming. And shit, maybe I am. If that car accident really happened, I *am* asleep. Just not the kind of asleep I thought I was.

Okay, not *if*.

Because that car accident happened.

......

"Do we have to do this in the bathroom?" I ask.

"You really want to talk about this in front of his friend?" Aminah questions.

"I thought you were ignoring him because you liked him?" I ask, trying to turn the tables on her.

"I was ignoring him because I thought it was really weird that you brought him here!"

"Aminah and I leave for school in a little over a month. Forgive us for being selfish and wanting to be around our best friend," Cameron says to me. She lays her head on my shoulder and pets my arm, knowing her guilt trip really stung me.

"It's our last summer. Let's not be wasting it on Michael Turrey," Daniel adds. "And Martin Fly or whoever. Yes, it's sad. Yes, you should feel bad. But no, you should not throw yourself into his life."

I salute him, opting out of words for fear of their inappropriate anger.

"Good. Now that we've settled that," Daniel says, "we need to come up with a way to kick Michael out of my backyard."

......

Somehow I'm in some gray, endless, nothing place between life and *you know,* and somehow I'm getting into people's dreams. Spencer and Turrey. And Petra. The girl on my mind when that car came barreling into my side.

She's dreaming of me.

I stood in the shallow end of a pool filled with strangers. They were yelling at her. Criticizing her for ruining their fun. I called out to her to let her know I was there, and she rushed over. In the weirdest way, she reminded me of my sister's cat. Like you could tell she pounced, but only when she had to, and never for more than she needed. It could've been the way she was positioned, balancing on all fours on the water's surface, her head cocked to one side, pain keeping her from relaxing.

The only thoughts I got out to her were "I'm stuck" and "I can't wake up," like they somehow summed up everything that's been happening to me. Whatever it is about Petra that makes her radiate—the glow stick she must've swallowed to make her burn so bright—was pointed in my direction. It lit me up too, and I swear she could see every single part of my entire being. Everything I really wanted to say disappeared. I wanted to deny that it was her dream or help her out of the pool so it wouldn't hurt her anymore or stop the people around us from yelling, but I didn't. I was like a caveman marveling at fire.

It does make me feel better to know *I'm* not the one imagining her in pain, but it hurts to know she's imagining herself that way.

I have to keep reminding myself: *it's not my dream.*

But it *is* my reality.

I can't forget that.

13

We sit in Daniel's kitchen, sulking around his island, already complaining about what's to come. We're momentarily ignoring the Turrey problem that was once so pressing I needed to be woken from sleep to address it. Hopefully ignoring the me problem forevermore.

"Our dorm room seriously goes from here," Cameron declares to Daniel, standing up to take a few steps forward, "to here. It's nuts."

"It's not that bad," Aminah says. She glares at Cameron. "At least we have each other. We could be living with a stranger."

This is one of those random transitional conversations meant to ease the tension of the fight we just had minutes ago. For them, it might be working. For me, a live wire has been cut, and it sparks around inside of me. Annoyance and Martin and algebra and scholarships and Martin and algebra and money and anger and Martin and scholarships and frustration and algebra and

Ryan and money and Martin and algebra and failure and—wait. Wait. No.

No Ryan.

Daniel gives me a look like, *Can you believe these two?* "You guys are the worst. I haven't even gotten my roommate yet. I could be living with an ax murderer." He keeps looking at me, expecting my scowl to rework itself into a pitying smile. "So could Petra."

"Well, I toured Notre Dame with Petra. The dorm rooms there aren't nearly as small as ours," Cameron adds. "If Petty Pet bunks her bed, she'll have plenty of room to hide from her ax-murdering roommate."

Now everyone is doing the thing where they use my name to get me to participate in the conversation. I know their hearts are in the right place, but for once, I don't care to pretend.

Guilt wears on me. For bumming around. For opening and closing the refrigerator door at my leisure. Asinine everyday behaviors usually taken for granted. All the things I do to avoid my problems. All the things Martin can't do at all.

Shirtless Turrey slides open the screen door before Cameron can ask me what's really wrong. The swooshing sound of his intrusion cuts through the invisible barrier my friends thought they hung in the air. This is what happens when you stop paying attention to your problems. They keep showing up.

"What's up in here?" Turrey asks.

"Cooling off," Cameron says. She offers him a cup, which he takes. He grabs the pitcher of iced tea sitting on the counter and begins pouring.

Aminah lurks by the fridge, shifting from side to side, her eyes skewering Turrey's every movement. "What are you doing here?"

Turrey puts down his cup. He maintains steady eye contact with Aminah as she fidgets. "Getting a drink."

"We don't know you," Aminah responds.

Awkward explodes.

Daniel somehow slipped out of the room. Even my detective skills missed it. Cameron and I, surrounded by the smell of organic kitchen-cleaning products and the draft of open windows, are helpless spectators to this unexpected face-off.

"I've been Daniel's neighbor my whole life," Turrey tells her.

"I've got lots of neighbors. Don't know the first thing about them. And there's probably almost six hundred people in our graduating class that I don't know either."

"Well, I know Daniel."

"That's doubtful."

"Is it?"

Quiet settles in. Aminah considers her rebuttal, squinting her eyes to see him in a new way. "Shouldn't you be with your friend at the hospital?"

It's a low blow, and we all know it.

I wince. Cameron winces. Aminah tries to stand tall, but her chest caves in.

"Maybe I've had a long twenty-four hours, and I just wanna sit by the pool and take a break for a second because one of my best friends could die, and I can't do shit about it." He sits down on the bar stool next to me. "I know I don't really know you guys. That's kinda the point. I can't be around my bullshit group right now."

Tasered by his words, Aminah fumbles for a chair, guilty.

......

Here's the simplest, silliest thing I want right now: my damn sandwich. Spitty has to buy it. He owes me. He let a car ram into my body. The least I'd expect is a sub.

Ugh.

I guess I don't know how any of this works. Am I waiting for people to go to sleep? Think of me? How much time has passed? Can I really let myself believe this is a real thing that's happening to me?

Mama Dorothy hates sleep. She thinks it's a waste of time. She probably doesn't use up any brainpower on dreaming. Maybe Dad. He's been a light sleeper ever since the back injury though. That man caught me every single time I ever snuck out, even the time I taped pillows to my feet so he wouldn't hear my footsteps.

Katie? Bet I'd get a good part in a Katie dream. What if it's a sex one though? The last thing I want is to be watching my sister get down with her husband in the bleachers while I'm stuck singing "Go Cubs Go." Why do I feel like that's what all her dreams are like? Horrific. I guess I'm glad I haven't had to deal with that.

Okay, that's a lie. I'd put up with my worst nightmare just to be able to let her know that I'm here. To let anyone know I'm here.

Where do they even think I am?

......

The single most valuable talent Cameron possesses—above good studying habits and being sentimental without being overbearing—is her ability to revive dead conversations. It must be eating her up inside that she hasn't figured out how to crack my sour mood because she goes overboard on Turrey. She drills him with the strangest of inquiries, playing on the innocence she knows she exudes, acting like she doesn't know anything when she has a pretty good idea about it all, but making Turrey both so confused and so filled with a desire to make her understand that he forgets there was ever a problem. Or decides it's easier to keep moving along. Either way, Cameron makes it work, and I can see in her swelling smile what joy it gives her. We listen to Turrey detail with great specificity what it was like to play two winter sports at the same time his sophomore year.

It shouldn't work, but it does. The tension wafts out of the kitchen.

It's rare for Aminah to embarrass herself. She wears the shame like a heavy cloak. For penance, she offers to make everyone a drink, digging into the pantry for a margarita mix and some tequila.

"I'm not touching that stuff right now," Turrey says.

"I can make food or something," Aminah adds.

"I'm good." Turrey nods. He does a finger point between him and Aminah. "We're good."

Aminah gives him a solemn nod in return.

"I'll take a drink," Cameron says.

"You're cut off," Aminah tells her. "The fact that you started an hour ago, by yourself no less, is sad enough."

Daniel is still missing in action. I don't interrupt the conversation—it's nice not to be the point of interest—to ask where he went. I just text him.

Where did you go?

> To my room

Okay
But why

> Too complicated to explain right now
> I told you guys we needed to make Turrey
leave!
> Find a way to make it happen
> Please

…Okay?
I'll try

Daniel Stetson doesn't usually miss situations like this. He is a long-limbed bird of a man, always perched in the spot with the best view of the action. Almost encyclopedic in his abilities, he can open the yearbook and spout off at least one thing about any of the 868. He's like a heart monitor, hooked up to the beat of our school, finding a thrill in documenting not only irregularities, but average rhythm too. Yet I can't recall a single time Daniel ever mentioned knowing Michael Turrey, even when we snuck into that Turrey family party.

"Oh my God!" I lead with, dousing the last word in urgency.

Cameron sways in her chair like she's now buzzed on my fake burst of energy.

I rub a space on my left index finger, as if plagued by a newfound vacancy there. "I left my...grandmother's ring at the hospital," I lie.

"What ring?" Aminah asks. Her left eyebrow arches. Suspicion replaces her last lingering bits of embarrassment. I'm not a jewelry wearer.

I opt to avoid her question, instead looking at Turrey. "Would you mind taking me back to find it?" I can both help Daniel and avoid dealing with my friends. It's perfect.

Aminah interrupts before Turrey can answer. "I forgot to say that Daniel thinks he broke his toe, and he wants Petra to go upstairs and look at it. She took a first aid class, so—"

She knows I'm lying, and I know she's lying, but we give each other our best poker faces, knowing Turrey is still an elephant in the room, and we can't let him in on the intricate dynamics at play here.

Turrey scrutinizes both of our features. He also knows we're lying. "Guess I should head back. Gotta be there for Fly, even if I don't wanna deal with everybody else. I'll look around. What kind of ring is it?"

"It's a purple square amethyst on a gold band," I make up, merging my birthstone with my mom's wedding ring.

Turrey finishes his iced tea, then pulls out his phone so we can exchange numbers. "Tell Daniel I was here," he says as he stands up to exit. He walks out the back door and grabs his shirt from the pool's edge.

As Turrey moves from Daniel's yard into his own, I call out, "I'll be back soon."

He turns back and gives me a wave.

"Pet-ra," Cameron says, slicing my name into two sharp syllables. "Will you please just talk to us about whatever's going on with you?"

......

Wherever this is, it's not the same as it was before. The grayness is changing. There's no thing, no place, no idea like this. It eats up all I see or feel the instant it happens, and everything that happens morphs into something else before I can figure out what came before. If I could hold on to the changes for more than a fraction of a second, maybe I could better explain. All I know is I'm becoming less. Or more.

Either my eyes are about to open or they are closed tighter than they've ever been.

......

"Daniel!" I call out. "The coast is clear."

Cameron sighs. "Hold on a second," she says to me. "I'm sorry we ambushed you earlier. We were just worried. Please talk to us."

The staircase creaks in a cautious way, steady steps tiptoeing down. Daniel pops out, wearing black swim trunks to match his black hair. He moves with suspicion, sizing up chairs and pantry doors for hiding spot potential.

"I swear he's gone," I tell him.

Daniel gestures to the sectional in the adjacent living room. "About time. Everyone take a seat, please."

"Hold on a second," Aminah says, repeating what Cameron said earlier but using a little more vinegar. "Something's up with—"

"Oh, something's up all right," Daniel continues. "Seats. Now."

We sit, one by one, Aminah tallest on the left with Cameron splitting the difference between her and me. We sink into the crinkling leather, our height leveling as Aminah slumps down in frustration and I straighten out in anticipation.

Daniel strides over and plants himself in front of the gigantic wide-screen. It creates a backdrop that outlines the slender tautness of his track-and-field physique. "Okay. As you now know, Michael Turrey is my neighbor."

I relax into my seat. For a split second, I thought he, too, might want to talk about me.

"Now you have a face to go with the home. Putting all that aside for a moment—" He makes a point to look at us one by one. "I have something I need to confirm for you all." He pauses for gravitas. "I'm gay. This is something I've known for a long time. Forever actually. Not sharing this with you was nothing personal. Just something I wanted to explore on my own while finishing high school. I don't believe any of you have ever had to declare your presumed straightness to me, so my proclamation of homosexuality is more of a courtesy. My graduation gift to you all," he says with a bow.

The three of us exchange looks while Daniel moves to a chair. We've anticipated this speech probably as long as Daniel's planned it, his steady delivery a dead giveaway of more than a few practice takes in his mirror. Not that any of us ever needed it confirmed to accept him. He's shown us in more ways than he's ever had to tell us, anyway. But the way he clears his throat, like there's more to the story, has all of us scratching our heads.

Daniel sits, living for our confusion, always appreciating an upper hand when it comes to secrets and big reveals. "Now, onto the *real* news," he starts. "The night before graduation, Michael and I got drunk on his roof. It's something we've done a few times a year since we started high school. Might've even started toward the end of junior high. I don't remember anymore. We sit up there with bottles of our parents' liquor, and we talk about whatever. Life. You know the kinds of conversations. Stargazing talks. We get drunk, crawl back in through his window. He passes out on his bed. I stumble home. That's how it's always been. Until the other night—"

My cell phone starts going off, one of the new constants in my life. The incessant vibrating has been very ignorable until now, when it's somehow so intrusive that we all hold our breath as it buzzes against my jean shorts. I fumble to silence it. "Keep going. Sorry about that."

Daniel absentmindedly strokes his forearm. I've sideswiped his storytelling momentum.

"Please. I have to know what happens next," I say.

"Fine. It was just getting good." He brushes off his arm and sits up. "Back to the other night. We're up there, chasing vodka with Mountain Dew. We finish up our talk and crawl in through his window. I go for the door. Like always. Michael stops me. He says, 'Just crash here.' I go to make a spot on his floor. He says, 'No. Stay up here.' I get into his bed. We're both lying there, staring at the ceiling, not talking. I can feel it in the air. Tension. The covers shift, and before I know it, Michael Turrey's on top of me." Daniel pulls the drawstrings on his swim trunks to make a popping sound against his skin. "And that's all she wrote."

"What?" Cameron screams. She's so loud she scares herself.

"Whoa!" Aminah yells.

"What happened after that?" I ask.

"I'm sure you can put together what happened after that."

"I still want to hear it!" Aminah pleads.

"Let's put it at this. Michael Turrey did not require a proclamation of homosexuality from me." Daniel winks. "I was drunk. He was drunk. I don't know what either of us was really thinking. Now here he is coming to my house all cozied up to one of my best friends, and we haven't even talked about what happened. He had to go!"

My phone buzzes again, just once. I pull it out of my pocket. It's a voicemail from Turrey. My mailbox is now completely full.

"Well, Daniel, I'm proud of you," Cameron says. She's beaming with tipsy pride.

"Please don't say things like that. You know I can't take it."

"Too bad."

"You need water," Aminah tells Cameron.

"We've got to find out what's up with Michael," Daniel says.

"We do. But first, Petra." Aminah straightens out, and her presence grows along with her height.

I throw Turrey's voicemail to speaker as a distraction. For the first two seconds, it's ambient driving noise. Then Turrey's unsteady voice. "Hey. I just got a call from Fly's sister. Shit's not looking too good. Fly's in surgery, and something's not going right. I'm still driving. I'll look around for your ring, but I probably won't be able to bring it back if I find it. Sorry."

14

Katie sobs in a gasp-for-air-dry-heave way. Her husband rubs her back. Turrey zones out. Brooke Delgado leans into someone's shoulder and cries. Spencer's dad clasps his hands in prayer. The other unidentified faces provide their own variations on those same reactions. Then there are us. Four ducks in a row, blocking the entry, kicking metaphorical rocks in contemplation.

"Do you think—?" Cameron whispers in my ear, afraid to finish her sentence. This is as quick as I've ever seen her sober up.

"I can't tell," I answer. "I hope not." I close my eyes and make a wish that everything will be all right.

With my eyes shut, a flash of a dream comes to me. I could walk on water, but it hurt me. Burned me. I was trying to escape the pain and find a way out of Daniel's pool when Martin appeared. He called out to me. I remember his face, which wasn't quite his, but still I knew it was him. When I reached where he stood, he said, "I'm stuck," and "I can't wake up." It looked like there was more he wanted to say, but he couldn't.

Then Cameron woke me up.

It's funny how dreams morph without notice, cutting out before you hit the ground from a fall or stopping right before a big reveal. Why couldn't I let myself understand what my version of Martin wanted to say? I must be trying to make sense of how a person's body can be alive but their mind asleep. Seeing Martin's eyelids flutter, knowing he's somewhere in there, but he's too battered to get out. He *is* stuck.

Yesterday, he was just the kid next to me at graduation. Lighthearted and goofy, working so hard to make me laugh that I started to forget how I'd sworn off boys. Now he's the focus of everyone's attention, all of us hoping against logic that he can pull through an accident that left half of him obliterated. Everyone in here must be clinging to their memories of him, afraid they could slip out of reach and become too distant to feel.

The alarming vigor with which Katie still weeps is both terrifying and amazing to me because it reminds me of how we are capable of feeling so deeply that it can torpedo through our very being. I bet she's thinking of how she used to punch Martin's arm when he annoyed her. Dare him to do something humiliating like eat dog food or hop the fence of the graveyard by the school. Katie must have had her own versions of all the power-play moves my older sisters had for me. Like any older sibling does, she probably exercised her power of seniority in between bursts of protectiveness.

Stone-faced Turrey must be wondering why he wasn't in the car.

Maybe Brooke is letting absence make the heart grow fonder. Everyone might know they aren't together, but now that Martin could be gone, every word he ever said or wrote takes on new meaning. Hormones get swapped for love in retrospect.

In a room full of retreading, mine is the weakest of all. I have less than twenty-four hours of reference to cling to, most of which was spent in this hospital constructing my impression of Martin through people who know him far better, making up a backstory and inner life for all of them.

But I might have been one of the last people to spend time with him.

My head and my heart don't know what to make of it, and I suddenly wish I'd just listened to myself when my inner voice said to stop while I was ahead. I never listen to myself.

I'm in so deep.

The four of us commit to finding a spot. Nervous shifting makes the vinyl seats squeak louder than the two TVs overhead. A dance of sorts ensues, each of us shuffling back and forth as we try to discern what Daniel wants to do about his proximity to Turrey. Boldly, he shoulders up to him, placing me in the next seat and Cameron and Aminah on the floor in front of us. They lean back into our knees.

Brooke wafts the dampness of her washed hair toward me, smelling like a Hollister store mixed with Herbal Essences shampoo.

"I'm Brooke," she says with an unthreatening smile. "I've been meaning to say hi."

I introduce myself, and through a nod she welcomes me as a comrade, much like Katie and Turrey before her.

"Can you believe any of this?" Her hands coax her phone into waking. The lock screen photo is one of her and Martin at prom in matching shades of orange.

"No," I answer, incapable of delving beneath simplicity into a situation so far beyond my grasp.

"Has anyone heard anything?" Aminah, the only one brave enough to ask, gently inquires.

"Someone came in and told us there have been complications. That was a while ago."

"Wow," I whisper.

The past two days of my life have been defined by waiting. Maybe all of life is defined by waiting. Waiting for food. Waiting for the bus. Waiting for test scores. Waiting for school to end. Waiting to graduate. Waiting to fix a problem. Waiting to fix the fix. Waiting to hear the fate of another person's existence. Waiting, waiting, waiting.

Death is just another milestone. Another thing we spend our whole lives working toward, waiting for, and it's all over in an instant. We're in a room designed solely for waiting, for building the bridge to the other side of something, and it seems that the little details that happen here, in between one thing and the next, are what define a life. So while I have the time, I'll define mine how I see fit.

Maybe willpower alone can erase all of my problems.

Brooke has no shortage of questions to ask me. How do I

know Martin? Where did I go to middle school? Who were my teachers? What classes did I take this year? How could we have both had gym fourth period? Who was my teacher? Did I ever see her there? Wouldn't it have been cool if we had talked then? Where am I going to college? Am I as nervous as she is?

My last two answers hiccup off my tongue. I want to think of nothing beyond this very moment. I want to keep waiting.

Genuine enthusiasm shines out through Brooke's eyes. Her ability to stay so engaged keeps me pulled inward, not wanting to give away too much too soon, stockpiling for conversations yet to come.

I think I understand how it works between her and Martin. It's as if I can see it as he would, piecing together what Turrey told me with what I'm experiencing now. She's stunning and charming and so free to share herself. So eager to know the people around her. So present in every moment. I see how that could make you love her, but it could also feel like too much in high doses.

She crosses her legs, and a flash of black ink pops out against the deep tan of her skin, just sneaking out from the hem of her leggings. "Real or fake?" I ask, my first attempt at being on the other side of the questioning.

Her eyes stop moving. Now they are still, gazing, almost startled. "You're the first person to notice since I got it." She tugs the legging down over the bumpy bone of her ankle so the ink is no longer visible. Before I can ask more, she's rummaging through her purse. "I do a good fake one though. Can I?"

She digs out a black marker with a thin tip and starts drawing flowers on my arm. I almost ask more questions. I want to know more about her and Martin, but she starts humming a soft tune to herself, and I figure the distraction is nice for her. Another way to survive the waiting. Her sandpaper voice, full of gentle runs and steady rippling vibrato, calms me.

Aminah and Cameron solve a magazine crossword puzzle with a startling lack of bickering, passing the glossy page back and forth with penciled-in answers, knowing they could use pen but not bothering to show off. Since we listened to Turrey's voicemail and rushed back to the hospital, they've become unreadable. They're waiting too. Waiting to find the right time to corner me.

Katie's crying dies out. Her husband pulls out his iPad and props it on his knees. They share a set of earbuds. She rests her head on his neck. What they're watching must not matter much. They both blankly stare at their handheld movie theater.

Daniel twists around pieces of my hair, avoiding eye contact with Turrey while still engaging him in conversation.

"How's your toe?" Turrey asks. "Is it broken?"

"False alarm," Daniel responds, tugging so hard on a clump of my hair that my eyes water.

Aminah told him her lie on the way over, and Daniel screamed for thirty seconds straight, almost turning the car around.

"I couldn't find your ring," Turrey tells me.

My arm jerks involuntarily, and Brooke makes a long squiggle near my wrist. "No worries. I think I just left it at home," I mutter.

Mr. McGee walks in, swallowing up every bit of space in my lungs on presence alone. The whole room takes a collective breath.

He walks over to Katie and whispers something in her ear. Her iPad falls on the carpet. They rush out of the room.

No one moves.

No one blinks.

No one exhales.

This can't be the end.

Martin can't be gone.

PART TWO

15

Spencer throws the White Whale into park and makes a break for it, sprinting around the side of the high school to reach the football field. An amplified voice projects names through the loudspeaker.

"Jude Banning," the voice calls out to light applause.

Spencer slows down. They're only on the letter *B*. He has plenty of time before it's his turn to be done with high school. The warmth of the sun against his face feels so good he stops and closes his eyes. The world burns red beneath his eyelids.

Red. Like blood.

Time hiccups.

Blood on Fly. Blood on Spencer. Blood on the pavement. Blood on his van.

Time jumps backward.

The White Whale cruises down a wide open side street,

nearing an intersection. Spencer looks to Fly, who doesn't have his hand out the passenger window like he should. What is he doing? Why is he staring at Spencer with wild, panicked eyes?

"I'm back," Fly says, marveling at his hands and body like they are new. "I'm back!" His excitement quickly changes into panic as he realizes where he is. "Spitty, stop it!" he cries out. "Think of something else!"

There is nothing else to think of.

Crash. Smack.

I killed my best friend.

16

P etra pilots an airplane built in the style of the Wright
brothers' initial conception. It's rickety and old-fashioned
on the outside, the color of dust. Inside, the technology is
greater than ever discovered. Petra is Amelia Earhart flying a
solo mission. Her innate skill for navigation makes her feel this
way. Invincible. The source of legends. A hero.

Dense foliage infects the center of the landscape, a dark
green cluster that could pass for mold growing on bread from
this high up. It's a bird's eye view, yet details that should only be
visible with binoculars are easily spotted, like brittle leaves on
gnarled branches twisting around clapboard homes. Minuscule
gaps between trees where the slightest sliver of paved roads and
man-made grass can be seen.

Petra can pivot and whirl as easily as if she were controlling
a video game, and she enjoys the weightless sensation akin to

whizzing downhill on a roller coaster. Her bottom never touches the seat, and her stomach tilts into her skin without any of the unpleasant jerks that come at the end of a decline.

If she's using controllers, they're operated with her mind alone, because the ones in her hand are decorative. She clutches one for effect, but when she thinks of turning left, she does. The handles don't move. Earth and sky alternate in view, tossing her in a washing machine of blended blue and opaque green.

She cocks her head, realizing in the midst of her intricate winding that she's forgotten why she's flying at all, and she hasn't paid attention to how close she's gotten to land. The head-whipping jolt of leveling out hits. She gets tossed into her useless navigation board. This machine she was once so in tune with has betrayed her. It's taken her too low, skidding along the tops of leafage.

Fighting against turbulence, she pounds on buttons, knowing that it's only a matter of time before her plane nose-dives into the great unknown, where the greenery will snarl around her as it has everything else. Rhythmic thuds rattle her as the plane bounces along. Down this far, almost inside the vegetation, she can see her parents wrapped in ivy, mere statues now, robbed of life. Her sisters Caroline and Jessica taken by the same fate. Cameron and Aminah and Daniel lie beside them, pinned to the earth by rotting branches. To her surprise, Turrey and Brooke are there too, their legs free, but their torsos tied up by vines onto something with a hint of yellow. A mailbox.

Petra gasps.

It's *her* mailbox.

Standing on a visible sliver of street in front of her yard, the ivy seeming to clear for him, is Ryan Hales, stretching his hands toward the plane to get Petra's attention. He's screaming something, his mouth making desperate shapes. But his voice can't break through the chaos inside the airplane. Not that she needs to hear him. She already knows what he's saying.

You're such a dumb bitch. Useless and dumb.

She remembers that she didn't want to see any of this. That's why she'd flown so high before.

Now, with alarming clarity, she can not only see it, but she's starting to feel it. The asphyxiation that took her family and friends has come for her, but there are no vines to wrap her tight. It's all in her mind. She screams for help, a plea so disparate from any other that it's only possible when one arrives at death's door.

"I can't go too!" Petra cries, thinking of how everyone she's ever loved is now gone. "Please."

She buries her head into her knees, imagining a world she can't crash into, one that would be a pillow to land on. She imagines taking the breath Ryan Hales doesn't deserve and using it for herself.

"No!" she screams, a rally cry.

Inches from the ground, darkness covering the panels of glass she once glimpsed freedom through, her plane swoops upward. A steeper incline than ninety degrees, she's almost upside down. The angle suctions her head back into the seat. Air, pure and whole and so strong it makes her cough, fills her body.

She's done it. She's stopped herself from crashing.

"Hey."

Petra turns. Martin sits next to her. "You're here," she says, surprised. She hadn't realized she'd saved them both. "I've missed you."

They're headed straight toward the ceiling of the world. There is only softness around them. Airy and puffy. Swirls of clouds, like tufted cotton, decorate the pale sky. It's a different fear now, because while Petra knows they're going up, she can't see anything in front of her, and the mystery of what is there waterfalls adrenaline through her system.

"Petra." Martin says it the way people do when addressing someone for the first time, testing out the correctness of a name by whispering it. "I'm stuck."

"You told me that before. In the pool." The past dream springs to her mind, and with that memory comes the thought of her life outside the airplane, where Martin's fate is not known. "Are you dead?" she asks Martin.

"No!" he says. "I'm stuck."

She's satisfied hearing it. She didn't want to believe he was gone. The plane keeps climbing.

"I think I was, though," he tells her. "I think I—died. It was exactly like going to sleep. Instant. Empty. Uncontrollable." He shudders. "But then, exactly like waking up, I busted back into Spitty's dream. Now yours." He stops and waits for her to turn. His voice is tangled and throaty. "I can't get out. My eyes won't open."

"You're not making sense," she says. Then she realizes.

"Because you're not the real Martin." Her waking brain is creeping in to interject rationality. She's starting to lose a grip on this world.

Martin becomes frantic, fighting against gravity to unbuckle his seat belt. "I am! I swear!" He tries to crawl. It reminds Petra of a ride that comes to the city carnival every year, the Gravitron. It's a circular structure that spins so fast it pulls you to the wall, and try as you might, you can't be peeled away. But Martin works against physics, somehow winning, making his way to her.

Waking Petra has a hard time allowing this to continue, skipping back and forth between the plane and a rigid couch where she lies asleep.

The airplane starts to level with Martin's every movement. "Listen," he says.

Back and forth, Petra slips from one world to the other, neither sturdy enough to fully support her. The plane flies forward. Uncorrupted white-bread land stretches on for miles.

Martin grabs Petra's shoulders. "Ask Spencer about the pact. Tell him the letters are in my closet. Top shelf, in an envelope inside the Foamposites box. He's the only one in the world, aside from me, that knows what that means. It'll prove I'm me."

Petra blinks, the first after a long sleep, the real world almost flickering into steadier view.

17

Whoa.

We return to our regularly scheduled programming: the grayness and the nothing and the feelings that aren't really feelings but aren't anything else.

Martin McGee here. Not gone but not back. Incapable of forming coherent sentences when caught inside the dreams of one very smart girl. Once again stuck in this place I'm going to call the Between, because it seems to be the blurry edge that separates life and death, a line where one world ends and another begins. A first-blink pressure that holds me right in the middle of both. I tipped toward one end but didn't fall all the way—which is good, don't get me wrong—but I'm really wishing I could've overcorrected, and y'know, woken up.

......

It is unusually cold—a crisp, steady, air-conditioning kind of chill. My heady is buried into a crevice. No blanket covers me. I'm not at home, I realize, shooting upright, panicked by unfamiliarity. I rub my eyes, hoping against logic that this uncomfortable vinyl couch will transform into my bed. The world comes into clearer view. Cameron's head is at my feet. Daniel spoons her. Aminah's sprawled out on the carpet below us.

That's right. We spent the night. This is the waiting room.

I rise up, tiptoeing over bodies to make my way into the adjacent bathroom. A mirror is on the wall, but I don't bother with it, too groggy to comprehend my face. It's too early. Or too late. My sense of time seems to be lost.

My mind keeps slipping back into my dream. I'm piloting an airplane. My family and friends are all dead. Ryan Hales is waving his arms at me.

Martin appears.

Martin is dead.

Martin says he isn't.

Ask Spencer about the pact. Tell him the letters are in my closet. Top shelf, in an envelope inside the Foamposites box. He's the only one in the world, aside from me, that knows what that means. It'll prove I'm me.

The words push me out of my liminal space and into the unnerving stillness of the empty bathroom. I flush the toilet and wash my hands with my head down, accepting reality but not needing to see my part in it.

A voice, one I know must be my own though I don't quite recognize it, as certain and steady as a line of permanent ink, emerges from the deepest parts of me, telling me my dream was as real as right now. Martin was there.

I need to find Spencer.

......

I died.

I can say it now. I'm past the point of being afraid. How can I be? It *happened*. I don't know how I know it, but I know. It's like when you say the wrong thing, but the other person plays it totally cool. It doesn't matter that neither of you acknowledge what happened. It can't be denied, no matter how much you pretend it's all good.

There was a phantom pain, and it grew stronger and stronger until it left me altogether.

I left myself.

I was gone.

Then just like that, I was back in Spitty's dream.

So I'm not pretending. I'm not trying to act like I'm making all of this up or I'm the one who's dreaming. Not anymore. I came back from dying. That means I have to fight.

......

"Where are you going?" Cameron asks me. She has on her favorite shirt, a gray tee with an ironed-on profile shot of a young Art Garfunkel. Freshman year we studied the symbolism in Simon and

Garfunkel's music for honors English. Cameron got obsessed and made the Art shirt, calling him her fellow redheaded-underdog-kindred-spirit-good-luck charm. It started out as nothing more than a laughable anecdote in a laundry list of her bizarre ticks, but with every A plus that came out of wearing the shirt, and every B that happened when she forgot, we've all started to believe in the power of Art, at least a little. She put it on before we left for the hospital. She'd happened to pack it in her swimming bag.

Looking at Art staring off in the distance and Cameron staring at me, all three of us in different states of deep contemplation, I agree to let her come along, giving her a nod in the direction of the door. I know she's dying to understand what's up with me, and it's all gotten so strange that maybe it will be okay to let her in on some of it. If ever anyone could appreciate the weirdness that's happening right now, it's Cameron in her homemade Art Garfunkel tee. She frees herself of Daniel's arm and joins me.

"What's happening?" she whispers as we begin walking. Even the hallways demand libraryesque silence. She winces at the fluorescent lights. "I have a headache. Why did I drink wine coolers in the middle of the day yesterday?"

"We're going to find Spencer."

"Why?"

It's too early to tell her I'm working on knowledge from my dream. I can already feel the details slipping, so to preserve what I remember, I explain to her about the shoe box and the envelope, saying Martin mentioned something about it at graduation. We go down on the elevator and walk through a few clickety halls before arriving at one of the hospital entrances. It's still dark outside. A woman arrives to sit behind the main desk just as we approach. She glances up. "Do you need help?"

"Yes, thank you. I was hoping to see Spencer—" I come to a stop. I'm sure I've heard his last name over the past two days, but it's nowhere to be found in the overflow of information clouding my brain.

"Spencer?" she inquires, as if I'm both troublesome and perplexing. The longer I pause, the wearier she grows. "Visiting hours won't start for a while, so I'd suggest—"

"Kuspits," Cameron declares. "Junior." Her unrelenting friendly smile bends the receptionist's will.

The woman plunks something into her keyboard, scans the information, and gives us directions. "I don't think they'll let you in!" she calls out as we head down the hallway to a new set of elevators.

"How did you know his last name?"

Cameron laughs, picking fuzz off Art's nose. "His dad left his wallet behind." I let out a startled gasp. "Oh stop," she says. "I'm planning on giving it back. I found it when I heard you go to the bathroom."

The elevator dings. We follow imaginary parallel lines inside.

"Why did Martin tell you that?" Cameron asks.

"I don't know," I say, and that's the whole truth. I don't know how or why or what it even means, but Martin keeps finding me, and I keep falling deeper. Away from my life and into the one he's left behind.

The blueprint for this hospital must read like a maze. It's a complicated series of turning hallways and elevator rides, all of which lead to places that look the same as what came before. It reminds me of my first week in high school, when I thought I'd never understand how to reach the east gym from the north wing, much less find my locker between classes.

Yet the desk clerk did not lead us astray. A nurse sees us walk up and looks like she's about to stop. Then she looks at a file in her hands like she hasn't noticed us at all.

Spencer doesn't have the luxury of a private room. In a space curtained off at the end of a series of similar rectangular setups, he's awake, reading a magazine. The first thing I note is the lack of flowers around his bedside. Martin's room was inundated. Then the bruising around his dubious eyes: a side effect of slamming into his airbag. Good fortune in comparison, because juxtaposed against what I saw of Martin yesterday, Spencer might as well have a four-leaf clover sprouting from the top of his brassy mop of curls. Aside from the bandaged broken nose and a gash on his forehead, he looks downright blissful, with a resting grin even tragedy can't seem to shake from his face. I remember seeing him at the ceremony. He's the one that told Martin to invite me to the party.

"You," he states, remembering me too.

"Me," I say, now knowing confidence is key in communicating with the Martin McGee crew. "How are you?" It's a useless question that I instantly regret, but words cannot be swallowed back once we've released them into the world.

"Been better." He looks to a clock on the wall across the way. "Kind of early for visitors."

"I know. I wouldn't have come if it wasn't important." That same voice, the one from the bottom of me, urges me to keep going, but another more rational voice tells me this is too far. I can't ask him about something from a dream. And a third—the voice that cannot be swallowed back—continues on with no notice of the conflict. "I'm sure you don't want to talk about what happened, so I just want to say I'm sorry, if that means anything. I'm here because Martin told me something." An uncontrolled note plunks out when I say his name. "He mentioned a pact. Something about an envelope in a Foamposites box. Said you'd know what that means."

The magazine almost falls out of Spencer's hands. Cameron instinctively clutches me.

"He said that to you?" Spencer asks.

My muscles are still seized as I try to do something that passes for a confirmation.

"Why would he tell you that?" he wonders, his gaze shifting upward, eyes darting back and forth, reading the blank ceiling tiles.

"I was hoping *you'd* have that answer," I say.

Cameron clears her throat to get his attention, but she only gains mine. Her quizzical stare shoots from me over to Spencer's hands. They are shaking, rather violently, and he doesn't seem the least bit aware. He is lost to whatever's playing out in his mind. Cameron and I observe, frozen in fascination, communicating our shared curiosity and fear telepathically. Neither of us wants to interrupt what can best be described as a memory exorcism. He jerks his head forward and locks in on me. "Can you get it?"

"The envelope?"

He doesn't answer. He goes back to wherever he went before he asked.

Cameron jumps in. "Of course! In fact, we will go right now! Feel better!" She shuttles us out of the room. Holding hands, we fall into a hallway corner. "That was the weirdest thing I've ever seen," she says.

I let go of her hand. "It's about to get so much weirder."

......

Petra's the one who showed me what it is to fight. In her dream, she screamed like Spitty did when the car hit. She said, "I can't go too."

Too.

Like someone had gone before her. Someone who she'd been thinking of a lot. Or at least enough to dream of three times. We were about to crash headfirst into this jungle that'd totally overrun everything until she screamed "No!" with so much force that the plane changed course.

It should've been over, but she fought.

And there I was, tongue-tied, trying again to explain just where it is that I am. Trying to fight as she did. Then it started. Dream skipping. If where I am now is inside a blink, what happened then was the action of blinking. I ping-ponged back and forth so much between there and here that I rushed through everything I wanted to say. For a dude who used to get yelled at for talking too much, I'm still no good at using the right words. There's so much I've never been able to say right. Or at all. But I got the point across before she tossed me back to here: my pact with Spits.

Grandpops died when I was nine. I'd never lost anyone before him. Adults tried to baby me. Katie was a wreck because she was there when it happened. My other friends couldn't relate. There was just Spitty, whose mom passed away the year before we got really close. He came to Grandpops's funeral. After the service, his dad dropped him off at my house to sleep over. All night we brainstormed a way to stop this horribleness from happening again. Neither of us understood how someone's body just stopped working. It made us so mad. You couldn't give us a person to love then take that person away.

Of course, we were a pair of nine-year-old boys. We thought there was an option of not dying at all. Actually, I'm pretty sure I thought that was an option right up until a vehicle smashed into my body on a sunny Friday afternoon in June. Anyway, if one of us happened to mess things up—go on and die—we created a plan for the other person.

We never talked about it again, but I know Spitty still remembers. That day bonded us forever. A pact, written on loose-leaf and sealed with a spit promise. A pact to keep us from hurting the ones we love.

......

"Why is it always more difficult on the way back?" I ask Cameron as we try to reverse our steps.

"It does seem to take longer. We should've written down what the woman said."

"No." I hesitate. "Never mind."

"What?" she asks, her tone teetering close to annoyance but masked with the perfume of her curiosity.

"Never mind!"

"Come on! You can't just start to say something then stop!"

"It's too strange to say."

"Great. I love strange things."

"Promise you won't think I've lost it?"

"Promise."

We both agree to turn left down a somewhat familiar corridor, reaching a new set of elevators.

"Martin isn't dead."

Cameron's finger hovers over the down arrow. "I mean—" She peters off, afraid to say what she's really thinking, which is that it sure seemed that way when Katie and her dad ran out of the waiting room. We all fell asleep waiting for news, but they never returned, and the nurses wouldn't tell anyone anything.

"The pact thing I said to Spencer—Martin didn't tell me that at graduation. He told me in my dream."

Cameron plunges her finger onto the down button. The doors open instantly, and we both enter, following the same parallel lines we did riding up.

"He said he isn't dead. He's just stuck. He thinks he did die for a minute, but he came back. Then he said the letter thing. Told me that would prove it was really him. And look how Spencer reacted. He couldn't believe I knew that." My words sound absurd once spoken, but however bizarre, they express my current truth. There's no denying the look on Spencer's face.

Cameron inhales for what must be the first time since I started spewing my fantasticality. "Does this have anything to do with what happened at Daniel's yesterday?"

"Yes. No. I don't know."

"Survey says for best accuracy, you have to choose one answer. *I don't know* is not an option."

"I didn't graduate," I whisper. The right answer to the wrong question.

Confused, Cameron falls onto the buttons inside the elevator. I stare at the illuminated numbers to avoid her gaze. "I don't get what you're saying," she says as she presses two again and again, hoping it will override the fact that she's also selected every other floor. "Graduation is literally the only reason we're here right now."

The earth shakes, pulling us down.

"I never took my Honors Algebra II final."

"Hornsby? Wasn't Daniel in that class with you? You were sick on finals day, but you went back the next week and took it. You got a C minus, and it murdered your GPA." Pressing two, pressing two. Pounding on two. Holding two.

"No, I didn't."

"But you said…"

The elevator stops. Doors open. Not our floor.

"You said…" she repeats, her voice getting smaller. She releases the two.

"I said a lot of things."

The doors close. Down we go.

"I have too many questions to pick one," she starts. Her breathing speeds up. She's picked one all right. "How could you be at graduation without a third math credit?"

I speak to the floor numbers. "My parents worked out a deal with the school. I had to go in and sign a form and all this stuff, basically promising to take the final with the underclassmen on Monday. *Tomorrow.* Wow, it's tomorrow," I realize, panicked for a moment. I shake it off. "If I don't pass, I have to take summer school, and I'll lose my scholarship at Notre Dame. Probably won't be able to go at all. But they let me walk because my parents were like *Caroline and Jessica blah blah blah,* and final transcripts don't get submitted until next week. It's a whole thing."

We jerk forward. The doors open. Still not our floor. I grab onto the handrail to steady myself.

She shakes her head, trying hard to comprehend this. "Why didn't you just take a math class senior year?" She squats down to try and catch my eye.

Tears have formed. If I look at her, they will fall.

Doors close. Down again.

"I don't know," I say.

I know, of course. But it's starting again. The words and the memories are creeping out of my attic and onto the main floor. Ryan's left hand is pressed over my mouth. His right is moving lower, probing.

Cameron hugs me. Her body works as a dam, stopping the

flow of memories from breaking me. "Eleventh in the class with a missing credit." She strokes my arm. "Steve Taggart probably carries a lock of your hair in his wallet."

I fake a smile for her. "Probably. He knows about the missing credit somehow."

"Leave it to Taggart."

"Enjoy your valedictorianism, Stevey. It's on the house." The elevator doors open to reveal a bright purple wall. Every hall on the way up was blue. "Ugh. What did I tell you about the way back?"

"Actually, you didn't tell me anything about it," Cameron says. Knowing she just successfully navigated us into and out of a delicate conversation, she doesn't press further. "We're going to Martin's, aren't we?" she asks instead.

"We have to now."

"You're right. This is so much weirder than I could have ever thought."

18

When someone dies, you're supposed to go through a series of feelings about it. Stages of grief or whatever. What do you do when you're the one that people think died? Telling Petra about the pact should get everyone to believe that I'm alive. Right? There isn't a soul in the world who knows about that aside from Spitty. You're not gonna get any better proof than that.

Right?

How long ago was it that I laughed this off and thought of it as one of my dreams? That is what is killing me, in the nonliteral sense. I have no idea. What if it's been like thirty years, and I'm some vegetable, and Petra's some freakin', I don't know, astrophysicist or something, and she's just having some random dream about that guy she met at graduation? Or worse, what if they buried me, and I'm suffocating inside my casket, and no one knows it and, and, and—

Shit.

What stage is this?

......

Wake-up-before-dawn Aminah tried to follow me and Cameron to Spencer's room, lost us on the way there, and then somehow found us on the purple floor. "Whatever you two are up to, I'm making myself a part of it."

Daniel and Turrey were both awake and deep in conversation by the time we figured out how to get back to the waiting room. The mention of a still-unexplained but exciting task was enough to get both boys to sign on board. And that's how Daniel's Prius became the unofficial Believe Marty Can Fly shuttle bus. Eco-friendly means space efficient, which actually means Turrey's right elbow in my rib cage and Cameron's left leg hooked over mine. Aminah managed to get shotgun without a single argument, which is no real surprise. The air seems to gets tighter when she wants something.

I don't mind. Close quarters are becoming more comfortable than distance.

Daniel taps his hands against the steering wheel. "I'm thinking now is a good time to tell us what we're doing."

"Going to Martin's," Cameron says. She adds a nod to encourage a normal reaction from the rest of the car, as if this is a logical place for us to go this early in the morning. Or ever really.

"What?" Aminah asks. She's been a little distant since she found Cameron and me. It seems like she could tell a moment passed between us, and it's probably eating her up inside that she wasn't a part of it.

"Why?" Daniel asks at the same time. Both of their heads jerk in unison to see me in the back seat. Before my mouth can open, there's a knock on the passenger side window.

I look past Turrey's hulking figure and see Brooke Delgado waving. "What are you guys doing?" she asks. Her words are muted by our glass barrier, but she enunciates every syllable so we understand.

Daniel mimes a sign of the cross. I lean over Turrey and open the window a sliver. This is another chance to get more information. I'm not passing it up. "There's room up front," I say.

"Looks like Michael should've sat shotgun," Daniel snarks.

Aminah opens her door. "Don't start."

Brooke snuggles in. The essence of her Herbal Essences has not yet faded. She forever smells newly showered. "I saw you guys leaving, and I followed. I've been inside this hospital for so long, I'm desperate for fresh air." She takes in everyone's faces one by one. Turrey twitches when she meets his eye. "Where are we going?"

"Apparently, we're off to Martin's," Daniel says. He catches my attention in the rearview mirror then breaks momentarily to glance at Turrey. I raise my brows to let him know I caught that. He looks away.

"Is that where his family went?" Brooke asks. Her seat belt hiccups as she tries to pull it across both bodies in the front seat.

"Sorry," she says to a grumbling Aminah. "It'd be ignorant not to be cautious."

"Six people in a car best for four," Aminah replies, the unspoken part of her sentence saying, *We're already ignorant.*

"If you knew anything, you'd know they're with his aunts," Turrey mutters.

Brooke continues radiating friendliness in our direction. She must not have heard him.

"Spencer asked me to check something out," I tell her. My cheeks warm from the heat of everyone else's confusion.

Brooke turns her torso toward the front of the car again. She flicks her wrist as if dismissing the mere mention of Spencer's name. "I hate him."

Turrey's arm muscles tense against my side.

"Couldn't even stay sober for his own graduation," she scoffs. "This is his fault."

In all the fuss, no one's talked about the why of it. At least not to us outsiders. I think back on Turrey's reaction to Aminah's offer to make margaritas. Spencer's hospital room. The lack of flowers. The nurse ignoring us.

"Fly was drinking too," Turrey says.

Brooke whirls back around with such ferocity that her hair flips into Aminah's mouth. "How do you know that?"

"Because unlike your fake ass, I'm actually his friend."

Daniel pulls out of our parking spot and rolls the windows down. Aminah turns up the radio until it's blasting. It doesn't help. Everything becomes so quiet that noise sounds like nothing at all.

......

All I can do is believe. I am a Cubs fan for Chrissake. My people waited 108 years for a World Series win. I know a thing or two about keeping the faith.

So I *believe* that time hasn't slipped that far past me. I *believe* that if I want to be back on the side of existence I've known for eighteen years, more than I've ever wanted anything, I will be brought back. I *believe* that I'm like first baseman Anthony Rizzo—game seven, bottom of the tenth—and the ball is a little high coming toward me, but dammit, I'm gonna catch it, because catching it means it's done, the curse is over; the Cubs win the World Series.

You know what? At this point, I'm not above skipping to the bargaining stage. Spitty didn't stop for the red light, but I was the one who let him drink and drive. I will take responsibility. Mama Dorothy's always telling me that when your chips are down, and you've really screwed up, sometimes a genuine apology is all you can give, because you can't go back in time and change what you've done.

So I, Martin Frederick McGee, am sorry.

......

Not a word, aside from Daniel's phone giving directions, has been uttered in the car since we left the hospital. As we unpack ourselves onto the driveway, we shake the cold silence out of our limbs. I step on a dried-up egg yolk. There are two more splattered onto the garage door.

In the early morning, when the night sky starts flirting with daylight's soft pinks, the McGee house doesn't look like the 1970s horror set I remember from Friday night. A garden in the front yard bursts with carefully maintained flowers surrounding a sign that reads *Welcome to the McGees!* Flanking the sign are four gnomes to represent each member of the McGee clan. Turrey's shoes crush tulips as he walks over to the little red-hatted man with Martin's name carved into the back. He picks up and drops the odd figurine in one swift motion.

"Are you for real, Spits?" he mutters, wiping egg yolk remnants onto his mesh shorts. "How can this kid be eighteen years old and still think it's funny to egg people's houses?"

When Cameron, Aminah, and I came to Martin's for his party, I noticed something sticky underneath my feet as we walked up the driveway, but I didn't think twice about it.

Turrey lifts the gnome up again, a two-finger pinch now, and removes a key taped to the bottom.

The rest of us migrate to the entrance. Turrey keeps the key held at chest level, a little bit away from him—a sacred object. The beginning of answers to questions not everyone knows they're asking. He parts the crowd to push the teeth into the lock. My heart is a balloon with a pin through it, waiting to be popped.

The front door swings into a clapboard hallway starved for light. A linoleum path leads into a carpeted living area straight ahead and a tiled kitchen to the right. Two staircases go up and down on the left side of the hallway. Shoes line the space between. From the first upstairs step, a backpack spills its contents out onto the ground. We stand facing this portal into Martin's life, our energy so stale it's decomposing. This is happening. We are here.

And Martin isn't.

Turrey positions himself in the center of the doorframe, blocking entry. One by one, the others turn to face me, slowly and deliberately, like a winning hand being shown card by card.

It's as if I've had my eyes closed and I'm blinking them open for the first time. Being silently confronted by this ragtag group of old and new strikes me as the most hysterical thing that could possibly happen. Nothing I knew of the world two days ago exists anymore. The gap between what used to be and what is just closed. I didn't mean to be, but I was standing in the middle of it all when it happened. It's the funniest thing. I laugh and laugh.

And then I'm crying.

I squat down on the concrete slab in front of Martin's front door, everyone else watching me as I laugh and cry like it's the most obvious marriage of emotions one could ever experience.

"Petra?" Aminah asks. "Are you okay?" She shoots a look to Cameron.

"I'm sorry to do this. It's just so funny. How I'm here. Why I'm here. None of it makes any sense at all," I say.

Brooke squats in front of me. Her eyes, constantly and beautifully water-stained, meant to feel everything all the time, try to send me comfort. "It's okay," she says as she holds my shoulders.

"No." I shift my attention from her glistening tears to Martin's backpack. "It's really not."

......

I'm sorry for always letting Spitty talk me into doing pathetic stuff I know isn't right. It's not like he'd cut me out of his life if I stopped doing all of it. Yet here I am, the sad excuse of a human who spent more than half of high school pretending I didn't like having my picture taken. Spitty was gonna give me three hundred bucks if I could go four years without letting someone get a good shot of my face. I got three years deep into this bet, ruining my sister's wedding photos, and I *still* lost, because Brooke started sobbing when I said I wouldn't take pictures with her at prom. Photos of me wearing a white suit with an orange-sherbet vest, orange-sherbet tie, orange-sherbet socks, orange-sherbet cummerbund, a top hat, and a cane are now the only semidecent ones my family's gotten in years.

It was all just a way to pass the time. Now I understand how precious time can be. There are much better ways to pass it.

I'm sorry.

......

"Pick your sorry self up off the ground, and let's do something about it," Cameron commands. She grabs my arm and pulls me up. "Ladies and gentlemen, we are looking for a shoe box with a letter in it. A pact between Martin and Spencer. Petra says Martin told her about it in her dream last night, and as impossible as that sounds, I believe her, and so should you all."

It might be for me sitting here on Martin's front doorstep crying, or it might be because they do in fact believe, but Cameron's unwavering certainty stuns everyone into complacent silence. Each face wears the same expression. For a beat, it's all there is to see. Puzzled sympathy coming at me from every angle. Even Aminah has no argument to make, and she never goes along with anything she can't directly fact-check.

Then Turrey moves out of the doorway, and every face drops to neutral, like curtains on the truth—back to the charade again. Cameron wipes dirt off my shorts and urges me inside.

Oh, how the air can change in a matter of two feet. It smells like laundry detergent and cigarettes and the sleepy warmth of mid-June. The linoleum creaks as I propel myself toward Martin's backpack. An unfolded note from Brooke sits in plain view.

> Fly,
> Honestly, I'm so done with this back and forth.
> I'm going to prom with Chris now.
> Brooke

It actually makes me laugh a normal laugh because I know that's not what happened. I saw their matching orange outfits on her phone.

Daniel and I wore black. His choice.

Brooke herself steps up behind me. There's tension in her movement. She must be conscious of the note. "I think it's upstairs. Maybe on the left?" she guesses. I look to the top of the stairs, but not before catching her snatch the paper up and shove it into her pocket.

Along the stairwell are portraits of Katie and Martin. Two ascending parallel lines, Katie's photos track her life all the way up through college and end with a photo of her and Rick from her wedding. Martin's stop on either eighth grade or freshman year, judging by his baby face and the tragic shaggy, surfer, bowl-cut hybrid hairstyle so many white boys have around that age. The blank spaces beneath Katie's photos—undocumented years of Martin's life—wait like sentences without punctuation. They lead to a door.

As I push in, Martin's world greets me with a new rush of the same pine-scented detergent I smelled downstairs. My eye is first drawn to the enormous picture of all these Cubs players hugging and celebrating, then the framed poster for *Back to the Future* that hangs beside it. I never got to tell Martin I was lying. Playing coy. It's Caroline's favorite movie. Of course I've seen it.

Sitting atop the tall dresser on the other side of the bed are a few trophies, a signed baseball, a poster for *Rookie of the Year,* and a picture of a shocked Katie in her wedding dress being lifted off the ground by Martin, his back to camera.

Brooke is beside me now. Both of us lean in the doorway with our heads against opposite sides of the frame. "I've never been in here before," she says. She walks over to the desk across from us and picks up the *SENIORS* hoodie draped over the chair.

Still as can be, like I'm holding a swatter tracking a fly, praying not to lose the chance to hit, I continue observing, as if what Brooke just admitted is no big deal. There's an elaboration to be made, I'm sure of it, and knowing what I do of her so far, she won't need prompting to give it.

A small lamp has been left on, casting light upward. It illuminates a wall calendar above Martin's desk. Every day is x-ed out up to this past Friday—the word *FREEDOM* scrawled beneath the final black mark.

"Turrey's right," Brooke says. "And so are you. It's not okay." Her finger circles Martin's last name printed on the back of his hoodie. "I've been so wrong."

A closet comprises the whole left wall. Its mirrored doors double the size of the space until I step into view and disrupt the illusion. "That's not what I meant." I almost reach for her but decide better of it, instead standing stiff-armed in the center of the room.

"I ruined everything." She puts the hoodie down but doesn't let it go. "I knew it too, but it seemed like something I could fix later. Like I'd have time. I know it's too late, but I'm trying to fix it now."

"I don't think it's too late," I say, but she's not listening.

"I never should've kissed him at Winter Formal. He was just being so nice to me. Why was he doing that? Boys don't do that. He let me talk about all this stuff going on in my life for, like, hours."

Hoping nonchalance keeps her spout pouring, I walk over to Martin's closet and slide one door back, finding rows of sneakers sitting atop their respective boxes on the ground. There aren't many clothes hanging up. The space is filled by a hamper and a bookcase crammed full of movies, old CDs, and tons and tons of books. Fiction, nonfiction, memoirs, sports photo books. A big enough selection to be Dewey-decimaled.

"We should've just stayed friends. He kept trying to go back to that, but I wouldn't let it happen. I guess I, like, wanted to break him for some reason. Make him like everyone else."

I freeze, locked in tight on her words, turning them over

and over like a coin. The absolute truth of it all takes my breath away. We do this to each other. We form mismatched pairs when there's nothing better around, then we poke and prod at every flaw, worming into hairline fractures until they become deeper. We dance on the destruction until the cracks cave in.

I force myself into movement, but it's taxing. I want to hug my knees to my chest and squeeze into a ball so small no one can ever get in again. Make myself unbreakable.

"I couldn't though," Brooke says. She comes over to the closet. "Even when I hooked up with one of his best friends. It didn't hurt him. It hurt me." She squats to look inside the shoe boxes on the ground. "I just want to tell him that I'm sorry."

I know I must speak now. Affirm that I've been here, hanging on every word, weaving together the final touches on my version of their relationship. "You'll get to," I say.

"I hope so." She reaches for more boxes in the corner of the closet. "Was he really in your dream?"

My breath hitches. "He really was," I say, as certain as Cameron. More certain than ever. In fact, this is just about the only thing in my life that I can tag with the word *certainty* and mean it.

Brooke looks up at me. "I like that you're here," she says. A moment passes. "Now did he say what shoe box it was in?"

I transport myself back to the airplane to hear his words again, feeling the weight of his hands atop my shoulders. Looking into his eyes. "Top shelf. Foamposites box?"

Brooke stands up on her tiptoes, looking right. I look left. It's so easy to spot it may as well be glowing. I step behind the door and grab it, pressing my back against the inside part of the closet, happy to be cloaked in darkness.

DO NOT OPEN. MARTIN'S EYES ONLY.

The sides are taped shut. My fingers work as gentle scissors to break the seal. When the lid lifts up, there is a sheet of loose-leaf paper taped over the box top.

I MEAN IT. DO NOT LOOK AT THIS.

I remove the paper. There's another piece beneath it.

PUT THIS BACK, KATIE!

The inside of the box is visible now. Against the perimeter, swollen with something beneath the surface, lies a rectangular envelope. I blink once, twice, making sure my eyes are focused. When I look again, I pick it up.

PROPERTY OF MARTIN MCGEE AND SPENCER KUSPITS
    TOP SECRET
                    ONLY OPEN WHEN DEAD

My back slides down the door, falling, falling, falling, until the ground finds me.

I'm sorry for letting Brooke kiss me at Winter Formal. She's an amazing girl. Any guy would be lucky to have the chance to date her. But her and me, we didn't quite fit. I knew it. She knew it. I guess you get to a certain point in high school where you run out of people in your circle, and you go for the unexpected. She's the most incredible girl I've ever been with, that's for sure, but we ended up being more like friends who sometimes did stuff then boyfriend and girlfriend. The whole reason she started hanging with me and the boys more was to get away from her other friends. Then word got out, and our "relationship" gave her a good excuse to stay away from them, so she ran with it. So did I. The whole thing got so complicated it seemed easier to just accept it. We played the parts well, but it never really felt as natural as it should.

Now I finally understand all the times she used to say, "I don't know. Buy me something random one day or something. I just want to know you're thinking of me."

Knowing Petra is thinking of me—that she's dreaming of me, over and over—it's enough to make a guy in a placeless place feel very much like he has a place.

But I can't seem to find a good way to tell her that.

······

I believed myself. I did. Martin was there in my dream. But this is different than believing. This is reality.

"Top secret! Only open when dead!" Aminah screams. She throws the envelope down as if it's contaminated.

Turrey picks it up by one corner. "Do we open it?" he asks, looking at me.

Like it was made just for this occasion, the McGees' dining room table seats six. I sit at one end, Turrey the other, and the rest in the seats along the sides, as if they're our children waiting for us to reach our executive decision. "Why do I have to make the call?" I shout.

"You're the psychic!" Turrey shouts back. He slides the envelope across the table. It collides with my folded arms.

"I'm not psychic! I'm just the only one who's been able to sleep!"

"Not true," Turrey says. "In my truck yester—" Disbelief strikes him in the face. "Fly was in my dream. Remember? I told you about it! Was it really him?" he asks, as if I'm an expert on this now.

"I don't know!" Yelling helps mask the quiver that vibrates through my whole body. I figured no one believed Cameron earlier, and I was right, because if anyone had, even just one, the force of that person's entire belief system being thrown into chaos would've crushed me. I feel it now, and air is so precious in my lungs I keep holding it in for fear that when it escapes, I'll never get anything back.

......

I guess what I'm figuring out is that I'm sorry for the ways I've hurt the people I care about. Maybe all we have is ourselves, but it's the people around us who lift us up and make us better.

Before Dad messed up his back, we did a cross-country road

trip every summer. I used to press my face against the glass and watch how, depending on how I looked at it, the outside world moved really fast or seemed to stay totally still. It blew me away. No matter what I picked, everything had to change eventually. Day melted into night. Flatlands grew into mountains. I liked it better when I took my time, staring at green grass until it morphed into sand or disappeared into concrete or something.

I don't remember when I started watching the blur. I stopped asking questions. Hated answering them too. They are tests I decided I'd rather not take. Brooke and her constant "Why are you being like this?" My dad and his "When will you ever do what you're capable of in school?" Spitty and his "What are you so afraid of, Fly?"

I danced across the graduation stage. I drank the whiskey. I got in the White Whale. And this is what I get. Just me, alone and filled to the goddamn brim with questions I can't seem to answer.

19

The doors swing out into a dark, expansive gym, skylights projecting moonlit shadows onto the squeaking lacquered floor. Basketball hoops hang from the ceiling, and banners decorate the whitewashed walls, detailing a select few of the tens of thousands that have laughed, cried, cheated, and lied their way through the many activities forced upon them in this space. Still the kids come back day after day, year after year. Even on nights like these—where laser lights cut across the floor in jagged patterns, x-ing over bodies swaying near the beat that booms from the speakers—they come by choice.

It's the Winter Formal.

Brooke searches the crowd for her date. She can't remember where she left him or why they've separated. Then again, he hasn't been much of a date at all. Not that she'd expected much. Though she did expect more than a wilted corsage from the grocery store and one obligatory slow dance at the start of the night.

Cutting in and out of the bodies—there must be hundreds—she wonders how it is she managed to find people to befriend in a school so large the gym can barely be navigated. Sweat has become an unavoidable accessory.

Frustrated, she frees herself of trying. Wherever her date went is somewhere he'd rather be. Why bother sharing the night with her? Apparently that's not why you ask Brooke Delgado to a dance. You ask her to get nice pictures and a healthy pat on the back from your friends. You ask her for the story, not for the company.

Apparently.

It's exhausting caring this much. Brooke pulls her shoes off her feet and holds them in her hands. Piece by piece, her expectations shift. If the only company she has is herself, she doesn't need to wear six-inch heels and pretend to have perfect posture. Her shoulders round forward as her bare feet strike the linoleum. Careful tears trickle down her cheeks. She will not let this ruin her night. She will give herself a few minutes to be bothered, then go back and force herself to have fun.

She wanders down a dark hallway, stopping and sitting when she finds a place far enough away that she can no longer hear the thrum of music pulsing from the gym. In this stillness a peace washes over her. She *likes* her own company.

It's his loss. And her friends' loss. They haven't even tried to find her. Or bothered to notice that she's looked sour and miserable most of the night.

"Brooke?"

Marty appears from around the corner. His white dress shirt is half untucked and his hair's a little longer than usual. The dance-hall body heat means the gel no longer holds it out of his face, so a strand flops on his forehead. He seems effortless and relaxed. Handsomer than she ever realized. She's so used to seeing him in baggy T-shirts and Cubs hats. But maybe she hasn't been seeing him at all.

Has she been asleep on Martin McGee this whole time?

Quickly, she brushes the tears from her cheeks. "Oh. Hey there. I couldn't find my date, so I figured I'd come grab some air." She pastes on a smile. "How are you? Having fun? Who did you come with tonight?"

Marty positions himself against the locker alongside her. He mimics how she's sitting, pulling his knees up for a place to rest his chin. "I hope you know how great you are," he says.

It's not what she's expecting to hear. In fact, she remembers it's not what she's *supposed* to hear. When they did this before, he told her he didn't come with anyone and he wasn't having much fun. They talked for hours.

Stunned, Brooke finds the tears do not subside. They grow stronger. "Marty," she whispers. "I'm so sorry."

He places a cautious hand on her back. "Aw, man, please don't cry over me. You don't need to be sorry. *I'm* sorry."

"Of course I do. I took advantage of you."

"Are you kidding me? Brooke." He grabs her by the shoulders, begging for her eyes to meet his. "I needed you this night just as much as you needed me. Do you know why I was out here? Because Chris was making fun of me for never having a date to the dance. Usually that shit rolled off my shoulders, but for whatever reason, I was believing him this night. I was, like, you know what? He's right. Nobody likes me like that. Then I stumbled out here, and you were crying, and I sat down and talked to you. I was just listening to you, thinking how could anyone be this shitty to Brooke Delgado? You know? Not trying to make a move on you. Not even thinking that was a possibility. Then *you* kissed *me*. It was surreal. You made me realize that people could like me."

Brooke laughs a little.

"I'm not even kidding," Marty says. "You really did. I saw that I didn't have to stop being me to get someone to care about me or whatever. Because I know I can be a lot. I'm loud and annoying and I try too hard to be funny sometimes. But this night, I was just being myself, and it turned out we were perfect for each other. For the night, at least."

"We really were," Brooke says. She leans her head on his shoulder.

"It was a lightning in a bottle kind of night."

"That we tried to make last for five months…"

Marty laughs. Brooke laughs. They both know it's true.

"Yeah," he says. "We really thought if we tried hard enough, we could make it happen again."

"But this night," Brooke says. "We got it right this night."

"Just so you know, I don't need you to kiss me for listening to you," he tells her. "I do it because I care about you. And I always will."

"Well, just so you know, I didn't just kiss you for that reason. Not this night."

"Oh, I know. I was just saying, you know, for the other five months of it."

A weight lifts from Brooke's shoulders. "But Petra?" she asks. She can feel his shoulders stiffen.

"I don't know—"

"Martin McGee, are you embarrassed? I never thought I'd see the day!"

"Cut it out."

"Hey, remember what you just told me," she starts. "People can like you. People can love you. People *do* love you." She presses her hands over his heart. "And we want you back."

20

Back to the hospital again. Before this weekend, I'd been here once: when I was born. The same receptionist from earlier in the day sits behind the main entrance desk. "Here again?" she asks us. "At least it's closer to visiting hours."

We travel as a pack toward the elevators, me at the helm, guiding us to Spencer's floor.

The envelope is in my hands. I grip it so tight that the sides start to fold over. Feeling the weight of it keeps me steady.

It is real. This is real.

We walk down a hallway lined with windows. Beyond the distraction of restaurants and stores packed along the roadside, the ground in the distance irons out, level and unblemished. It appears to be an edge, like if we headed toward it we would fall off. Maybe that's where Martin is. The place where the round Earth turns into an edge. Somewhere impossibly possible.

Not dead. Just stuck.

Everyone stares out at nothing as they walk, tracing back through the last two nights of sleep and wondering how it's possible that I know what I know.

Brooke is especially off her guard. She fell asleep on the car ride over, and when she woke, she had a startled look on her face, like something happened she wanted to discuss but didn't know how. She kept looking back at me, her lips slightly parted, words failing her.

I understood anyway.

She'd seen him too, but she's not sure how to take that and carry it with her into waking life.

I used to love the idea that in sleep, my mind could form a narrative around ideas from days, months, even years prior. Something as unsubstantial as dropping a piece of paper could get put away for later use. And the feeling, that punch-drunk, knee-buckling sensation of waking up from a great dream so complete and whole that you spend the rest of the day peeling imagination off reality; that used to be my favorite escape from the madness that was school.

But last year my dreams started to brown at the edges. Slowly they rotted all the way through, and every time my eyes closed, one single memory multiplied against itself. I taught myself not to pay too much attention to my dreams anymore. To wake up and purge them from memory without a second thought.

It's some unspoken human code that we are to be bored by dreams. We are to think they don't matter. I've tried to believe that. I've never been able to, even with all the trying in the world. Now, for the first time in a long time, my dreams have done some good. I don't know how or why, but the voice that lives in the deepest parts of me confirms it, nodding yes when everything feels like no.

It's the worst possible timing. A reroute at the end of a deadline I've been limping toward for a year. The final is tomorrow, and I'm holding an envelope instead of the thick study packet collecting dust on my desk. The anchor in my stomach shifts around, just to remind me that it's there.

But I need this, I say to the sharp pain that comes after the anchor settles. *I need to help Martin. I need to feel like* maybe *can become* yes.

When we arrive where Spencer is, the nurse from earlier this morning approaches us. "He's read every magazine we have," she says. "He fell asleep a little while ago and woke up very upset. Won't close his eyes again. Maybe you guys can help distract him." She leads us to Spencer's bedside then slips away.

Spencer coughs in response to the sight of the six of us. It must be strange to see this group glued together by the accident he caused.

"Didn't think I'd see you here," he chokes out, looking at Turrey. "Chris said you've been off doing your own thing."

"You don't look too bad," Turrey says. They clasp hands. Nothing about it is right. It's just a formality. In some ways, it seems like it's an insult. "Damn." Turrey shakes his head. "I told you guys not to drink."

Spencer takes it. No rebuttal. Not even a reaction.

The edges of Martin's envelope have started to fray from my iron grip. I can see loose-leaf paper inside. "We got this for you," I say.

It leaves my hands and goes into his, and he slips his fingers underneath the edge. He pulls out three sheets of paper and begins examining them. A question mark hangs in the air for so long it numbs the rest of us into placidity. Just six people staring at one person in silence for what seems like forever. Abruptly, Spencer drops the sheets and looks at the ceiling tiles.

I gesture to the papers splayed out along his side. "May I?"

"I don't care," he says.

Novemember 12

Dear Marty or Spitty,

It is Marty and Spitty. We are 9 years old. This is what you do if one of us dies. We will haunt you if you do not do this! You have to do this to who is dead, Marty or Spitty!

1. Make sure I am dead. Please look at my body and really make sure I'm not sleeping.

2. You can have all my good stuff if I'm dead. Give away all my other stuff so my family isn't sad.

3. Tell my family to stop crying and be nice.

4. Give them my note.

REMBER! REMBEMBER! REMEMEBER!
THE DEAD ONE WILL HAUNT YOU IF YOU DO
NOT DO THIS.

Sinserly,
Martin Frederick McGee
Spencer Alan Kuspits Junior

......

Everything happens for a reason. Brooke got that tattooed on her ankle the day after her eighteenth birthday. I sat with her in this divey parlor in the city, owned by her cousin's friend's uncle or something, and waited as she picked out the type of writing she wanted. It looked like it was going to be a bust. She blew through two books of fonts without any luck, and she didn't want the tattoo guy making something up. She looked off into space, holding her head up so tears wouldn't fall, and she saw this random picture fixed to the ceiling that said something like *Persistence Overcomes Resistance* in weird, scraggly cursive.

"See? Everything happens for a reason!" she screamed as she pointed to the picture.

The tattoo guy grabbed a ladder, took the picture down, stared at it for a while for reference, made a draft on paper, and then went to work outlining *Everything Happens for a Reason* on Brooke's skin. All ten of his knuckles were inked with the words *TRUTH* and *KARMA*, which seemed to be pretty perfect for the occasion.

"Are you sure you want to do this?" I asked.

"Yes," Brooke said. Her grip on my hand got so tight I thought she might actually break bone, and the guy hadn't even started tattooing. My hand was numb by the time he did. I distracted myself from the possibility of permanently losing feeling in my fingers by staring at the needle making a million little pulses into Brooke's ankle, the sentence she chose getting covered up in black smudge, then wiped clean, another word popping out to be read for all of eternity.

We stopped at her favorite ice cream spot afterward. She was licking the edges of her Rainbow Cone to keep it from dripping onto her hands when I asked, "Why'd you get the tattoo?"

She'd been so secretive about the whole thing earlier it felt like I'd set off a bomb if I asked then, but her mood had since taken a complete 180, so I figured it was safe.

She told me that when she was twelve, her brother died not far from where we were parked. He was outside trying to fix a broken spoke on her bike when a car spun out and crushed him.

She came to our school the next year, and all of her brother's stuff got thrown away in the move, so she couldn't find anything that he'd written on to use as a reference for her tattoo. She was ready to give up on the whole idea when she saw the handwriting in the picture on the ceiling. It was exactly like she remembered her brother's.

"I guess I don't get it," I said. "His death was an accident."

She put her ice cream cone in the drink holder and shook her head as she wiped multicolored drips off her shirt. "Yeah."

"But the tattoo," I started. I didn't know how to continue. None of it made sense to me. How is there a reason for a fluke like that?

"Exactly," she said. "He lived for a reason. A million of them, of course, but one was to always look out for me. He died for a reason. To teach me to never take a single second for granted. Now I have a permanent reminder of that."

I wanted to understand, but I just didn't. There was a reason for his life, but no reason for the way he died. He was a victim of being in the wrong place at the wrong time. I remember thinking if that happened to me, and my brother got killed while trying to fix a goddamn bike, the last thing I'd want on my body was something that said there was supposed to be a reason for that.

If I accept the permanent ink on Brooke's skin, this mantra so many people seem to chant whenever things go wrong—that everything happens for a reason, that I was meant to get into a car crash, to be here now—shouldn't I be able to see what the reason is?

When I was in Brooke's dream, I tried speaking honestly. Owning the truth of what we were to each other. That wasn't the trick, either.

So what is?

......

I pass the first page around and read the second.

November 12

Mom and Dad and Katie,

Go on a road trip to visit my aunts and uncles. I'm dead but I'll come because it will still be a good time. I'll win every game of I Spy, and nobody can get mad because you won't even know I'm cheating. Sorry, Katie.

Please don't be sad. I hate when Katie cries. I don't want my mom to cry. I love her very much. I've never seen my dad cry so he'll probably be okay I guess. Katie told me Grandpops smiled when he died. You guys can smile now. I miss him very much, so I know you miss me too but Grandpops smiled because he was happy. You can be happy too. Give some of my stuff to Spitty. He can have my books. Let Turrey have my shoes. Chris can have my candy wrappers or something.

I liked being your son and brother. Rembemeber that and do not be sad or mean! Tell the Cubs to win the World Series for me. That is my only request. Also, ask them to play "Jump" for me and my dad. Dad can sing it very loudly like when it comes on the radio in the car or when he cooks bacon on Sundays. He has a bad voice, but he likes to sing when he is happy. I like to sing that with him.

Please be nice. You were a very good family.

Love,
Martin Frederick McGee

Spencer comes around from his state to snatch the last paper from my hands. "You don't need to read mine," he says. Then he looks at me. Really looks. Hard. It's a focus he hasn't displayed since I met him.

"I didn't find out about these letters the way I told you," I admit. I tell him about my dreams.

As soon as I finish explaining, he scowls at me. He doesn't believe. His heart wants to, I'm sure, but he's too damaged to listen to it. Instead, he lets angry words flow out of him. It seems that he might be trying to scream at the world for being so senselessly cruel, but only random fragments are coming out, which just elevates his frustration. "He told me to stop thinking of it! Tell me how I'm supposed to do that!" he yells as he grabs at his hair.

I look around for help. There isn't a nurse in sight.

"Hey!" Spencer yells at me. "Don't look away." Now his words make sense. "You think you can help? You don't know the first thing about anything."

I try not to react, but it doesn't matter, because he moves on to berating Cameron for "standing around and acting like she knows me too."

Brooke for "sleeping with Chris before prom and still going with Fly."

Aminah for "crossing her arms like that."

We all look at one another, puzzled, working hard to not feed into his frenzy.

Spencer moves on to Turrey. "Wipe that look off your face," he says, smiling so big I can see most of his molars. "You think you're so much better than me because you weren't in the car. Guess what? I know the real reason you didn't come with us after graduation."

Daniel and Turrey fidget at the exact same time.

"Exactly," Spencer says in response. "I saw you guys on your roof." He points to Turrey. "You knew I was coming to egg your house on Thursday. It's tradition. Did you think I skipped you on accident?"

Cameron grabs my forearm. Her palm is slick with sweat.

"I parked my car because I was trying to figure out what you were doing," Spencer continues. "I thought maybe you were waiting up there with eggs you were gonna throw back at me, and I was actually pretty impressed. But nothing happened. You guys went in through the window. You didn't close it after. I got out to throw my eggs inside your room, because how epic is that? Would've been my best work yet. And I heard you guys." He pauses. "Yeah. *Heard.*"

"So what?" Turrey responds. "I like guys. Big deal. I know you're not about to try and make me feel bad about it."

Brooke starts looking around the room, trying to find someone to share in this news with her, but we're all too focused on what's happening.

"Daniel's not the reason I didn't want to leave graduation early, so you don't know what you're even talking about," Turrey continues. "Maybe I wanted to give my mom and dad a hug for always being there for me. Maybe I wanted to celebrate the fact that I'm black and I made it out of high school alive. Maybe I knew your sad ass would do something you'd regret." He nods. "Yep. It's all three of those things."

Spencer looks down at his hands. It's stone-cold silent. Like a *get nervous to think anything because you're afraid your thoughts can be heard* kind of silent.

"You can't try to hurt us worse than you're hurting," Turrey tells him. "It doesn't work like that."

Like the flick of a switch, Spencer starts sobbing. Almost convulsing he's crying so hard. He can't breathe out of his nose, but he keeps reaching for it to wipe snot away then remembering it's too tender to touch, frustrating himself more. "I'm sorry," he says through the constant stream of tears. "I don't care that you're gay." His eyes scan over the rest of us. "What the hell is gonna happen to Marty? I can't lose him. I can't." He hiccups over his tears. "I can't. I can't. I can't. I can't—"

This continues for so long that two nurses come in. They give us looks that say, *Please leave.* As we walk out, the racket from Spencer's room quiets, like he's been put to sleep.

PART THREE

21

The parking lot is full. Spencer's 2002 Dodge Caravan sits a little crooked from a hurried park job. White with black detailing, like a color-inverted orca, the White Whale calls him over, oval headlights keeping constant eye contact. *Why aren't the eyes of a killer whale where they look like they should be?* Spencer wonders to himself. Then he laughs.

It doesn't matter. Everything is perfect. He is free.

He climbs into the driver's seat. Fly gets in on the passenger side. The two amigos are supposed to be on a joy ride inside the White Whale, just like they've been doing since the end of sophomore year when the driving gods finally let Spencer pass the driving test, and he talked his dad into letting him inherit this beautiful beast, which had been rusting in their driveway since his mother's death.

But Fly isn't having it. "Spits, come on," he says. "We don't have to do this."

Spencer ignores him. He takes two travel-size bottles of whiskey out from his glove compartment. He bought them with his fake ID a few hours ago, making him late to his own graduation. The guy at the liquor store didn't even pretend to care that he was supposed to be a twenty-nine-year-old Floridian named Josh. He passes one to Fly and takes the other for himself.

Spencer chugs his back in less than four seconds: a new record. His tiny bottle clanks against the black tar of the parking lot as he tosses it out the window. He's never done this before. Left evidence on school property.

It doesn't matter now. Everything is perfect. He is free.

"Spitty, listen," Fly says. His voice cracks under the pressure of his own intensity. "I'm trying to wake up. You can't keep bringing me here. When that car hits me over and over, *I feel it.*" He throws his full whiskey bottle out the window. "This is all a dream, Spits. Think of something else. Think of us in Chris's kitchen trying to teach his grandparents how to use Snapchat or something."

Spencer revs up his engine and throws the gear into drive.

He's got the windows down. No music. No need. The sound of high school ending is the best sound in the entire world. There are no other cars on the roads around the school, so Spencer presses down on the gas pedal. He looks over, disappointed to see that Fly doesn't have his hand out the window. He's not wiggling his fingers around to grab the niceness, as if it can be held. He's not saying, "By the way, that girl's coming tonight." He's not doing what he's supposed to do.

"You're really missing the point," Spencer tells him. "Don't you know I was joking when I threw that paper airplane? You didn't actually have to ask that girl to come. Will you ever learn to take a goddamn joke?" Spencer presses harder on the gas pedal. The adrenaline will wake Fly up. Make him remember that it doesn't matter. Everything is perfect. They are free.

"You don't mean that," Fly says.

"Oh really?" Spencer answers. "And how do you know?"

There's a small black blur behind Fly. Spencer thinks it's a bug. Maybe it's a bird. It could be a car.

A car.

It's a car.

Spencer can't get his mouth to catch up to his mind. The words, "Fly! Look out! Look out!" come out eventually, but it's far too little and way too late. His foot jumps over to the brakes on instinct, every ounce of energy inside his wormy body channeled into his right foot.

The car smashes into the passenger side. Into Fly. Forward and sideways forces combine to slam Spencer into his airbag and door. His head collides with the heavy pillow of the bag and the glass of the window, breaking his nose and jumbling his brain. He can find only one thought. *I killed my best friend.*

Crash. Smack. I killed my best friend.

Crash. Smack. I killed my best friend.

Spencer's head hits the airbag over and over, the point of impact replaying on a constant loop.

22

Again and again and again and again, the other car devours my arm and my leg. Smushes my guts. Pulverizes my lungs. Shatters my body and rearranges the pieces into something unrecognizable. Every time my bones get crushed, the shock of the pain doesn't shut me down. Wanting to stop Spitty's dream becomes the only thing strong enough—real enough—to keep me from surrendering to the hurt.

Still, crash after crash, I can't change a thing. It's like his dream and his memory are welded together into something more powerful than I know how to handle.

......

The lights in the hospital cafeteria are so unforgiving that every dark circle and blemish seems to be not only obvious, but accentuated. It doesn't help that everyone's already wearing sour looks.

Spencer's breakdown cast a fog over us, made worse by lack of good sleep.

We carry our trays of food and find a table. It isn't difficult—the hospital's not very busy and the cafeteria has just opened for the day—but still we choose a corner, as if the lights will be kinder to us there.

"I'm absolutely starving," Brooke announces, trying to kick-start a conversation.

"Me too," I say, both because its true and I don't want to leave her hanging.

The others give halfhearted nods and start scraping at their plates.

We sit awhile in this lull. I devour my food without looking up. The others are probably doing the same, but I don't give myself the chance to find out. It's nice to wrap myself up in the monotony of something as simple as eating, especially when the rest of life seems to be a full-time tornado.

Out of nowhere, Brooke blurts out, "By the way, I think it's great that you're gay." She looks back and forth between Daniel and Turrey as if they're one singular unit. Her expression is so earnest that it makes the whole thing funnier than it has any right to be.

The darkness loosens its grip on us, just enough to let the barest hint of smiles creep onto our sallow faces.

"Thanks, Brooke," Daniel answers. He pauses to arch his eyebrow. "I'm also a Sagittarius. And genetically predisposed to hating cilantro. Let me know if you have any feedback on this."

It can be hard to withstand a Daniel Stetson jab. To her credit, Brooke doesn't break. She cocks her head and raises her eyebrows. "Your loss. My abuela is an amazing cook. I'd hate for you to miss out on anything she makes with cilantro."

My phone buzzes in my purse. It's become such a constant sound that I've learned to tune it out completely. I only hear it now because Aminah is rummaging through my purse in search of it. "This is like the sixth time in a row. At least put the thing on airplane mode if you're going to ignore it this much," she says. She pulls it out and declines the call, then pulls up the menu. "Here, I'll just put it on Do Not Disturb. That way it'll still ring, we won't have to hear it, but they won't think you're dead or something."

Her slip stills the table.

"Has anyone heard anything else?" Cameron asks, even though we all know the answer. Her attempt to help Aminah out of the awkwardness is valiant but unsuccessful.

We go back to picking at our empty plates.

Spencer's dad rushes into the cafeteria. He has his hand on his forehead and his eyes squinted in concentration.

"Mr. Kuspits," Turrey calls out. It's a relief to have another human to distract us.

"Oh, Mike, hey," Mr. Kuspits answers, releasing a held breath. As he walks over to us, he doubles back and checks under chairs and beside garbage cans, looking for something. "I lost my wallet. I've been everywhere in this damn building trying to find it."

Cameron holds my arm. "Shoot," she whispers, sheepish. "I have it, Mr. Kuspits. I've been trying to find you and return it."

Mr. Kuspits cries out in relief. "Thank you! Losing it was the last thing I needed. Where the hell did I leave it?"

"In the ICU waiting room."

He nods. "Ah. Yep. That's what I thought." His shoes click faster against the floor. Cameron hands over his wallet. She takes a deep breath, ready to explain herself further, but he just tucks it into his back pocket without a second glance. "Did you guys hear the news about Marty?"

Anticipation flips over all the new food in my stomach. Brooke grabs my hand.

"We just got back," Turrey tells him.

"You were smart to head home for a while. A doctor didn't come talk to us until ten minutes ago. Got about twenty people camped out here, and you take that long to give us information? Not how I'd run things." He throws his hands up in the air. "They said Marty flatlined during surgery yesterday. They got him back, but they wouldn't get more specific about how long he was out. Now I think that's strange, but hey, I'm not the guy in charge." His hands go up again. "They're saying something about brain bleeds and brain damage. They're looking into how bad it is. Marty's still unconscious." His face falls, as if the meaning of what he's said finally registers. He rests his hand on the table, trying to continue but the words seem caught in his throat.

His reaction reminds me of my dad. The need to be informed and keep everyone else informed too. The criticism of incompetence matched with the implication that he could do it better, while also knowing he'd never try. The emotions held way beneath the surface, only drug up by the most extreme circumstances, and even then, never fully breaking through. To know one guy like my dad and Mr. Kuspits is to know all of them, as much as you possibly can know a guy like that.

My phone lights up in my hands. It doesn't make a sound, just as Aminah promised, but it's ringing. And of course, it's my dad. For the first time all weekend, I answer his call. I don't know why. Impulse distracts me from reality. Only after I put the receiver to my ear does it occur to me how odd a choice it is.

"Petra! Where the hell are you? You haven't been home since yesterday morning," he barks into my ear.

"Sorry, Dad," I say, mostly so everyone knows who I'm talking to, "I've been at the hospital."

He makes a gargled noise as his concern and anger fight over who gets to talk first.

"One of my friends got into a really bad accident," I tell him before he can choose a victor. The same thing that happened to Mr. Kuspits happens to me. Speaking it aloud makes it hurt.

"We saw that on the news. You need to get home. Right now."

23

I s anyone home right now?" Michael questions.

"Shouldn't be. My parents are out," Daniel answers. Excitement fogs up his thoughts. It's happened before, and it's finally happening again, sober and clearheaded.

It's decided. That's where they go. Where they were before can't be said, for it's too vague to be anywhere. Daniel opens his front door, and Michael follows, the silence between them so loaded it is certain to combust.

Daniel's front room is spacious and airy. All furniture available, asking to be occupied. All the buildup, and now they're here. Daniel falls into Michael, kissing him like nothing has ever mattered more. He pirouettes him down the wall, not even bothering with the couch. Tender and passionate all at once, it's everything Daniel's ever hoped for in a romantic encounter. A boy from his own school. It's a first, and it matters more than all the other hookups he's had, because beyond knowing, there is friendship. Beyond friendship, there is tension. Beyond tension, there is possibility.

Daniel slows down, taking a moment to look at Michael. Something new and unfamiliar reaches out of Michael's eyes and into Daniel. Trust. Daniel uses it as a signal to lift up Michael's shirt. He places it on the ground with care. He kisses Michael, soft and slow, shutting his eyes to take it in. When he pulls back, ready for another step, the front door creaks open.

The two boys part. Daniel expects to find his parents gawking. Instead, his hodgepodge new friend group awaits them: Aminah, Cameron, Petra, Brooke. And Martin?

Is this really the famed Martin McGee?

Daniel can't be certain. He has only a hazy idea of what this boy looks like. But there's a certainty he feels. There's no way this is anyone else.

The group takes in shirtless Michael Turrey and flustered Daniel Stetson. It's certainly a rare sight.

"What?" Daniel asks, trying to regain his signature blasé composure. "We're a little busy here."

His confidence eases a laugh out of everyone. Even Martin, who's standing there looking mystified. "Do I know you?" Martin asks.

"Excellent question," Daniel quips. "Do you?"

"Well, I don't know. I'm here."

"I think that solves it then. Now would you mind leaving? I love you all, but really, I'd like a moment."

24

This is gonna sound so strange, but I keep thinking of what it's like to hug my mom. How she smells like cigarette smoke in a bakery. Her loud-ass voice hollering for the home team at every sports game. The number one fan of being a fan.

My dad. The man who eats Cheerios religiously because my mom told him it would help with his cholesterol. I'm pretty sure he doesn't even have cholesterol issues. He's just like that. He looks like a guy who listens to NPR while reading the business section of the newspaper and drinking a latte, but he loves classic rock and drinks two shots of whiskey every night before bed. He does read the newspaper though. He refuses to get information from the internet. I love him for that.

God. I really do.

Spitty and I have a hundred-dollar bet that Katie will name her firstborn Wrigley, boy or girl. I mean, I get it. Dad raised us to live and die by Chicago sports. If you wanted in with him, you had to love every team, but the Cubs most of all.

Katie's more than that though. She's a great listener. I can't even count the amount of times I've complained to her about the silliest things, and she's always interested. She'll be like, "So is your Spanish teacher still giving you weekly detentions even though you weren't the one to draw penises on your homework?" and I will have to think for a good twenty seconds because she'll be following up on a story I told her months ago.

What a good sister.

The best sister.

Then there's Spits. The curly bowl cut he hasn't changed in ten years. The braces I swear he's had for even longer. If he ever gets them off, his teeth will probably have little white squares stained onto them for the rest of his life, and he'll have no place to store the extra pieces of his sandwiches. Speaking of, I still want my graduation sandwich. He owes me a Potbelly's Wreck with extra salami now. And a cookie.

No. Two cookies.

Dammit, Spitty.

Then you've got Turrey. That kid—a lifelong White Sox fan—got me a custom Cubs jersey for my sixteenth birthday. That's the nicest gift I've ever gotten in my life. It's so Turrey of him. Low-key thoughtful as hell without being showy about it. He works his ass off to be good at everything he does; sports, gift giving, being a friend. And he makes it all seem easy.

And of course Brooke, the girl who sat behind me in freshman biology and used my arm to draw pictures of protons and neutrons and electrons. Who gave me Mina Lonigan's number sophomore year and told me exactly how to ask her out, then gave me a heads-up the day before Mina was going to break up with me. Who stood up for me that time Hornsby thought I was cheating on my test, when really, I was just trying to find my lucky pencil. Who wanted to know me even after kissing me.

Rounding it out is Chris, the guy that's in the group because he's never been anywhere else. I love him for that. It's comfortable. It's what we know. It's how life has always been.

But now the gallery of all the people I love shuffles through my memories on repeat. My feelings for all of them are so strong it's like I touched a hot stove and I can't take my hand off. It's a constant ache that I can't place because it's pain that is physical without any physicality, because I don't have a body, because I made some extremely terrible choices. I hate all of this so much. I don't want some untouchable idea of pain. I want the real thing.

I'd love a paper cut right now, and that's really saying something.

Dreams are like movies. When you're in them, your focus is pulled to the star. And there I was inside a dream starring a dude I didn't recognize, and he was with Turrey. Like, *with* Turrey.

So now someone I've never met is dreaming of me. Some of my friends are his friends. One is more than just a friend actually.

Up until Friday, my life always felt like enough. Like my heart was at capacity, and I didn't need to find any new people to know and love. Now my list seems way too short. I can see all the spaces between—the experiences I hid from, the people I never really let in.

I see how their lives are getting fuller just by knowing one another, and I'm just here, stuck, watching it all happen without me.

······

Ever since the first day of high school, when Daniel sat in the open seat at our table in Honors Biology, it's been the four of us. Now Cameron and Aminah sit in the front of his car, Daniel and me in the back, and I notice the spaces between us—the experiences we hid from, the people we never really let in. I see how it doesn't matter as much as it seemed to in school. We've been gone from them for ten minutes and I already miss the way Turrey and Brooke filled in the gaps. We blended into their group without protest. Or they came into ours. There isn't even a difference. We're all trying to survive the same thing: the waiting.

"Thank you for everything," I say to my friends in the car. Against their better judgment, they have been here for me this weekend.

"You know we love you, Petty," Cameron says. She rubs her palms on Daniel's steering wheel, having driven for him so he could get some quote unquote "beauty rest."

"*Tell them,*" she mouths to me through the rearview mirror.

Aminah laughs. "What were we gonna do? It was come with or not see you. I swear, you're twenty times stubborner than I am." She turns to touch my hand. "And I mean that in the most loving way."

"Please don't let it get sentimental in here," Daniel coughs out.

I didn't even realize he'd woken back up.

After a beat, he lets out an exaggerated sigh. "Okay, fine, I'll be serious for a second. I need to thank you guys too. For being patient with me. I know you've known about me forever. There was a time sophomore year when I was convinced Petra had found my secret Tumblr account with all the queer fan fiction I'd written."

I did find that, but I don't say anything.

"Thank you for not pushing it," he continues. "And not being weird about the Michael thing."

"Of course." I can barely pause before my curiosity barrels over my politeness. "Can we know what's happening?"

Daniel tosses a forlorn look over his shoulder. "Well, when you all left for your little mission to find Spencer the first time, you woke me up. I go to follow you guys and see Michael looking—no, staring—at me, and I think, 'This is so ridiculous. I need to know what's going on.' So I ask him. He doesn't lie. He says he cares about me. He's just trying to figure out how to be brave like I am." He stops for a second, amazed. "Isn't that funny? He doesn't know that I came out to you guys literally yesterday. He said he was scared of what people would do to him—it's not easy being black and gay—but he was also saying that with all that's happening with Martin, he doesn't want to run out of time, because what if it's all gone tomorrow?"

"So you're together?" Aminah asks.

"Kind of. I'll be at college soon..." Daniel drifts off, much closer to hitting a nerve than he prefers to be. "Part of me knows it's going to have to end when I leave, but I also can't stop myself. I like him." He rolls down his window. "Sorry!" he yells over the wind, waving one hand back and forth like a broom. "Have to air the car out. Can't have sappiness polluting my Prius."

"Keep the window down because I have one last thing to say," Cameron starts. "You *are* brave. All of you. And I love you all."

"Jesus, Cam!" Daniel screams. "They don't make a Febreze for this!"

Nervous spit gathers in my mouth when Cameron pulls into my driveway. "I'm dreading this," I admit. "I wish I could just fast-forward through it. Or somehow go back in time and stop everything from happening in the first place. That would be nice too."

"You'll be fine," Cameron says. She's doing her best to be assuring, but hitting only false notes. She knows, like I know, that a storm is brewing.

"Hey, what if one of you comes with me?" I ask. "That way my parents can't kill me for going MIA."

Aminah shrugs. "Sure."

"Really? I didn't think that would work."

Cameron starts to protest, but Aminah's already out of the car and walking up to my front door. I lean over and give Cameron a hug. Then I wrap my arms around Daniel. "Thanks again. I'll text you guys soon."

Daniel pretends to claw at my arms. "Can't. Breathe."

I open my door and linger near the passenger side of the car. "Do you think Martin's going to be okay?" I ask Daniel in the interim.

He just looks ahead—neutral, unreadable. "I think whatever you think."

"Yeah," I say with a nod.

Cameron climbs into the passenger seat, and Daniel moves to his rightful place behind the wheel.

"Did you at least have a good little rest? Catch any sight of Martin?" I joke as he readjusts the driver's seat.

"Ha," he says, like it's just a word, not a reaction people experience. It's so weird I start backing away from the car. I think he *did* dream of Martin, which is as cool as it is surprising.

I wonder what Martin thinks.

"Good luck," Cameron says as I continue my puzzled tiptoe toward my house.

My dad opens the front door before I even have a chance to search for my keys.

"Hi, Mr. McGowan!" Aminah says cheerfully.

"Aminah," he responds with an awkward head bob. He closes the door behind us. "Petra's mom and I need to have a talk with her in private." So much for my plan to have a friend diffuse the situation.

"I'll be in your room," Aminah tells me. She disappears up the stairs.

I follow my dad into our kitchen and find my mom sitting at the head of the table. She doesn't even get up. I've been gone for a whole day, my friend is dying, and she doesn't even hug me. Dad sits down on the other end. They flank the table like Turrey and I did at Martin's just hours before. Now I'm relegated to the role of obedient child along the side.

"So," my dad starts.

"There's not much to say right now, honey," my mom finishes, even though I know there's quite a lot she'd like to say. Her voice quivers. "If you're acting out because you're scared—"

"Please stop," I say. Unexpected anger pipes into my voice. I want to get this over with as quickly as possible. "I know what this is. You think I've been off rebelling. Showing you I'm not like Caroline and Jessica, who by the way, was the one to give me a ride yesterday and conveniently didn't tell you where she'd taken me. I'm not acting out. Everything is so different than it was on Friday. You don't even know."

Mom rings her hands. She's wearing her speech-giving face. She's been known to talk for so long that you forget what you wanted to say in the first place, so I keep going before she makes me lose my train of thought. "Mom, Dad, thank you for wanting the best for me. For trying to keep things on track when everything got weird at the end of last year, and for working with the school to figure out a way to fix it. I am truly sorry I continue to screw things up and make you guys look bad."

We McGowans don't like to stare truth in the face, especially when it's ugly. We pretend to care about what we deem important, but we don't actually look. We accept the surface, acknowledge the flaws, then put all of our energy into never going an inch deeper. It used to be an easy way to live. But the axis of my universe has tilted, and the things I tucked away long ago fall out of hiding without warning.

"There's so much that matters more than the studying I know you're about to tell me I should be doing," I say. "But for your sake, I'm very sorry." It feels neither good nor bad to speak the truth. It exists in the gray area I've been thrust into by Martin's accident.

My parents look at my face as if it's uncharted territory they aren't sure they want to discover.

"You never even asked me what happened last year," I start, the words falling out. I'm on fast-forward all right. My feelings fly out without a chance to filter. "You saw a problem and went and made a solution without ever checking to see if I was okay." I sound the way I feel. Sharp and unsteady. "Well, I wasn't. And I'm not. Now you're the ones who want to talk. And I don't. It is what it is. I'll take the test tomorrow, and we'll forget all of this ever happened."

"Petra," my dad says with the stern edge I know means I've gone too far. "If you're going to act like this, I don't want you in my house."

"Honey, you can't be serious," my mom says to him.

"She doesn't get it. I know there's a lot going on, but I can't listen to her act like a scholarship isn't a big deal. We pulled a lot of strings to get them to accommodate you."

My chair makes a loud dragging sound against the wood floors.

I stand up and walk out.

25

Spencer cannot believe how pathetic Fly can be. He's already got a Brooke Delgado problem bigger than the White Whale, and here he is going for another hometown girl. When will Fly stop being such a sucker? Spencer grinds his foot into the gas pedal. The Caravan wheezes before it takes off. Spencer looks over to see if the speed is making Fly freak out.

Much to his surprise, Fly looks as serious as he's ever seen him. "Spencer," he says. *He never uses Spencer's real name.* "Stop it."

Time jumps backward.

The two boys are now walking through the quiet parking lot, headed toward the White Whale.

"See!" Fly exclaims. "I knew you could do it." He turns around. "Don't get in the van. We already know what happens when we do that. Let's walk a while."

"What do you mean?" Spencer asks. What could be better than cruising down empty streets, feeling the wind blow in through open windows, knowing high school is over? He fishes his keys from his pockets and unlocks the door. Inside the car, it smells like White Castle and weed. Like bad decisions and good memories. There is nowhere else he would rather be.

Fly stands outside the vehicle, arms crossed over his chest, his ridiculous yellow graduation robe bunching up into his armpits.

"Dude, stop being like this," Spencer says. "C'mon. I've got two more bottles for us." He opens his glove compartment to fish them out, wiggling them at Fly to entice him.

Fly doesn't budge.

"I don't know what the hell you're doing, but you're starting to piss me off." Spencer turns the ignition over. The White Whale roars to life.

"This is a dream," Fly tells him.

"You're right about that," Spencer answers. "We graduated, we have alcohol, and Chris didn't rat us out for leaving early. It's damn close to being the most perfect moment of our lives."

"Spencer, *think*. Just a second ago, we were past this moment, already driving, then we jumped back to walking. Explain that." Fly presses his forehead into the passenger window. "We got in an accident. And I haven't woken up." Something stuns Fly. "Wait, shit. Did *you* die?" He shakes his head. "No. Petra would've told me that," he says.

Spencer laughs so hard he almost chokes on his saliva. "Were you smoking before the ceremony or something?"

Time hiccups.

Crash. Smack. I killed my best friend.

Time returns to the scene outside the car.

"Spencer!" Fly pleads. "You can't tell me you didn't just live that."

Spencer leans his back into the headrest. For a moment, the world was noise and blood and regret. Squeaking tires and grinding metal. Forward and sideways forces slamming and crunching and crushing. Fly is right. This *is* a dream.

But it's also a memory.

Spencer remembers now. He turns his head as if submerged in jelly—slow and cautious—afraid to spook the current reality away. He sees him standing there—Martin Frederick McGee, his best friend since that kickball game in second grade. The first person he called when he found out he got into ISU. The guy who's supposed to stand beside him when he gets married.

Fly's still got his forehead pressed into the passenger window. A red dot is forming above his eyebrows. A condensation circle grows on the dirty glass. His eyes are swollen with fear, but still, somehow, hopeful.

"Why did you tell Petra about the pact?" Spencer asks. It's all he can think to say. How can Martin McGee look so hopeful while acting on the very thing they designed around lost hope?

"I had to prove it was really me. It was all I could think of."

"Why didn't you tell her how you got the scar above your lip or something?"

"I don't know. It's not like I have a lot of time here. Dreams are weird, man."

They almost laugh. In another circumstance, they would. But they can't now.

"They say you flatlined on the table," Spencer says. "Now they're saying something else is wrong. Brain bleeds and stuff."

Fly opens the passenger door and climbs in. "Whoa."

"Yeah."

"I'm sorry," they both say in unison.

"Petra's trying to help you," Spencer says. "She came to see me. Get this—she was with Turrey and Brooke."

"That's why," Fly says, realizing something.

"What?"

"In Turrey's dream, she was there. And in Brooke's dream, Brooke knew about her. I didn't even realize then how strange that was. And then I was in some kid's dream I'd never met at all. I think he's Turrey's boyfriend."

"Yeah," Spencer says. "His name is Daniel. They're all friends now or something. Turrey's dating his neighbor."

The two boys sit in the stillness. Words seem trivial.

"Petra's more help than I can be," Spencer admits after a while. "I can't think about this stuff when I wake up. It makes me too sad. But I'm gonna try to be helpful. I'm gonna tell them you're still in there."

"What are you gonna say? *Excuse me, Doctor, Martin McGee's brain is fine. He told me so in my dream.*"

"I don't know. Petra pulled off the whole dream thing pretty well."

"She also pulled off that graduation robe," Fly jokes.

Spencer nods as Fly tries to find a smile. It's the best they can do.

"I'll find a way back to myself," Fly assures him. "I know I will."

"But how?" Spencer asks. He notices a black dot behind Fly, growing closer.

They're driving.

When had that begun?

The black dot looks like a fly. A fly flying at Fly!

No.

It's a crow.

No.

It's a *car.*

Spencer can't get his mouth to catch up to his mind. The words, "Fly! Look out! Look out!" come out eventually, but it's far too little and way too late. He presses on the brakes as hard as he can.

Forward and sideways forces combine to slam Spencer into the airbag and door. As his head collides with the heavy pillow of the bag and the glass of the window, breaking his nose and jumbling his brain, he can find only one thought.

I killed my best friend.

Time cannot be stopped.

26

B ut how?" Spitty asked. How will I find my way back to myself?
If my brain is bleeding and my bones are broken, how
is it even possible?

There's something to the fact that I've always been Marty in
the Middle, comfortably lost inside the center of things. Rise
to the top of the class or fall too far below, and people take
more time to look at you. The only time I've ever really pulled
apart from the pack is the time I got in a car crash and started
to die.

Oof. That's some truth right there.

So how do people rise to the occasion? They grit their teeth,
and they keep moving, in whatever way they can move. A forward
step isn't always physical, but it's momentum, no matter how far the
destination. There's trust in that process. That if you keep going,
you'll get there. I mean, I'm apparently uniting friend groups.

That's not something I'd ever think myself capable of accomplishing. So I *am* doing something. I think I'm doing all I can.

How do I know if I'm doing all I can if I've never done it before? If I've always settled for the middle?

......

While we wait for Daniel and Cameron to pick us back up, Aminah sits beside me on the curb just beyond my house. She's painting her nails the same color I've chipped off my fingertips all weekend, resting her hand on the stony concrete while balancing the bottle between her thighs.

"That didn't go well," I tell her. My body belies the calmness in my voice. I'm shaking.

She lets out a casual laugh, shrugging a piece of hair out of her face as she does it, trying to stay focused on her hand. "I figured as much when we went storming out of your house like we were being chased."

"I couldn't stop myself. I called my parents out for caring more about my grades than me."

She blows on her left hand then shakes the polish bottle, preparing to paint the right. "Welcome to the club."

I bite my tongue until she elaborates.

"My parents told me I had to be out of the house by graduation. Yes, like out, as in I don't live there anymore," she answers, always a pro at anticipating what question comes next. "I left last week. They aren't the biggest fan of Aminah Prabhu, girl without plans for the future. Right before I left, they sat me down and reminded me my first name means trustworthy and my last name means God, basically. But no pressure, right? I think this is all part of a bigger lesson they think they're teaching me about the"—she puts up air quotes—"*real world.*"

"But you and Cameron are going to U of I together."

"I'm just living with her. She paid extra for a single room. It might not work, but we're going to try." She closes up the bottle and tosses it into the backpack she haphazardly threw together before I came barging upstairs.

"Wait, you didn't get into U of I?" I can feel the axis tilting farther, spilling out debris from wreckage I'd failed to notice.

"I didn't even apply."

I'm so stunned I have to remind myself to take a breath.

"You look like Cameron when she found out. Her face was purple. She calmed down eventually. She came up with the plan."

"It's not a very good plan. Or very legal, if we're being picky," I note. "Why didn't you apply?"

"Oh, I know it's an awful plan, but I love her for trying, and I don't have anything better currently." She stops to look at me. "I don't know, Petra. I'm just not ready to go to college yet. Or ever. And I think that's *my* choice to make. Not my parents' choice. But they won't let me live at home if I don't go, and I don't have any money to support myself right now, so I'm hitching a ride on the Cameron Catherine Elizabeth Hannafin-Bower express. It's as good as I've got right now."

"How did I not know any of this?"

"We've all been off in our own little worlds." She examines her unpainted hand. "Isn't it funny? We all know each other so well, but every one of us has been keeping a secret or two."

She's right. Daniel with Turrey. Aminah and Cameron with U of I. *Me with graduation. Me with Ryan.*

"I think it's because sometimes you've known someone for so long you assume they know how to read your mind," she continues.

She's right. It's always felt like they know everything there is to know, through my moods or the words that I don't say. But sometimes, no matter how long you've known someone, you have to spell things out.

"Kind of funny considering there's a comatose boy wandering through everybody's dreams," I try to joke.

......

When it comes down to it, I'm just a comatose boy wandering through everybody's dreams. Spencer set the script of his dream in concrete, and it dried long before I showed up. No matter what I tell him or ask of him, he keeps going back to the moment everything changed.

There has to be a better way. Not shock. Not denial. Not anger or bargaining. Not trying to send messages that might not matter when the person wakes up. The harder I fight this invisible war, the harder it becomes. How backward is that? I might be letting a car slam into me over and over, and gaining nothing but a memory so powerful it becomes all I remember about myself. My ideas about who I am and the life I've lived for eighteen years—they're all I have here. If I lose them, I lose me.

What is it that they say about quicksand? If you don't resist, it's easier to get out. Maybe I move by not moving.

So I'll become the gray I live in.

Become nothing at all.

......

"Would ya look at us? Quite the band of misfits and rejects!" Daniel says.

"Excuse me," Cameron huffs. She's about to elaborate but decides better of it, instead reaching for her water bottle and taking a pronounced sip.

"You are not exempt, Mrs. Garfunkel."

Cameron puts down her drink. She brings her finger to the window and starts drawing on the glass. It's too bright for her—or me—to see what she's doing, but she continues. "Remember the thing you said about the way back?" she asks me.

"I knew you wouldn't let that go."

"Of course not. I was thinking about it while you were gone, and I think I figured out what you were saying. It's like, you climb a mountain, and the whole trip up, you have a goal. See the view. Then you get there, and it's beautiful, but there's nothing to work toward anymore. You have to go back to where you've already been." She turns to me. "High school was our mountain, obviously."

"Isn't Mrs. Garfunkel particular poetic today?" Daniel sings out.

"You're just jealous you don't know what I'm talking about."

He throws his arms up. "Guilty."

"Hands on ten and two," she scolds. "Anyway, the journey changes you. Even though you end up at the beginning again, you're a different person than you were when you started. We

193

were too focused on the view on the way up. Our climb back down's been really weird so far, but look at the plus side. We have new friends for the first time in, like, ever."

Aminah shrieks. "Enough of the mountain thing. Plus, that's not even true. I've had many exes that you guys banished from our trail." She slaps her own wrist. "Dammit, now I'm doing the mountain thing."

"Don't even start on your tragic exes. That is a detour we don't want to take." Daniel pulls into his driveway and shuts off the car's engine. "Mountain joke intentional. But also the end of the trail." He pulls his fist from the sky to his chest. "And scene."

"Well, what about Petra and Ryan Hales?" Aminah spits out before she can stop herself. She clamps her lips so tight that Ryan's last name comes out as a gurgle.

Daniel fakes gagging. "I thought we agreed to never speak of the dark ages again."

I simmer in the moment, preparing to let it pass, but find my mouth opening instead. "You all know what really happened, don't you?"

......

......

It's been quiet for an entire minute. I counted. Sixty whole seconds of stonewall silence outside of Daniel's house. I say, "There's no good answer. I know."

Another thirty seconds tick by. I say, "I don't know why I said anything."

Fifteen seconds. I say, "It doesn't matter."

Five seconds. "It definitely matters," Aminah says back.

......

......

My axis isn't tilted anymore. It's upside down, and every hidden truth I have knocks into the next, into the next, into the next. I can barely stay far enough away from the domino effect to keep breathing. "I don't know what's happening to me. I promised myself I'd never bring it up."

"You don't have to talk about it if you don't want to," Daniel says.

For me, the most hurtful memories always feel like a fifty-fifty mix of pathetic and powerful. "Who told you?"

"Sometimes Ryan would be in the locker room when I got out of track practice," Daniel whispers.

Bile, tasting like venom, mingles with my spit. "I hope you know he never got me. He didn't win."

"Oh, I do," Daniel tells me. "He told his friends that you bit his hand. That's the only reason I didn't go ballistic on him straight out. I knew you'd already gotten the better of him. But just so you know, I stole his gym shoes on his last day of school. And I tripped him. It was the least I could do for you."

One single laugh shoots out from my gut, followed by spurts

of little chuckles, the pathetic side of the hurt appreciating the powerful side. It helps. It's a battle for control that's festered inside me for an entire year.

"That's my girl," Aminah says to me. "Biting his hand."

Cameron hands me a napkin to use as a tissue. She contorts her face into a sympathetic scrunch. "I'm sorry. We'd try to bring it up, and you'd shoot us down. I never knew what to say. I still don't, if I'm being honest."

"You and me both." I close my eyes, fighting against the memory as it tries to resurface. "Don't feel bad. You're right. I never let you guys bring it up."

"We still should've tried. I'm bad at this stuff," Aminah admits. "I hate him."

"Let's kill him," Daniel says. "I know. Too soon. I'm obviously terrible at this too."

We shift and squirm underneath the wiped tears and deep exhales, searching for a way to make it all better.

"So yeah," I say to break the mood, letting out a small laugh even though it isn't funny. "There's also this other little thing. I didn't graduate."

Daniel and Aminah laugh like it's a joke they don't get but know that they should.

"She's serious," Cameron affirms. "She's supposed to retake her Honors Algebra II final tomorrow."

"Hornsby? What do you mean? I took that class with you. You were sick, but you went back and—*ohhhhhh*." Daniel spins his finger around an imaginary globe. "It's all connected."

Aminah stretches out the word *what* like taffy.

Our verbal conversation has at least ten different body language conversations beneath it. The entire car is an opus of movement: confusion covering fear, squeezing nervous, tracing circles into the jeans of baffled.

"Have you even studied?" Cameron exclaims. Her face is flushed with urgency. She just put this part of the puzzle together.

"No." I look down at my shoes. My oldest sneakers. They're caked with dirt. I guess they've been this way for a while, but it's now I choose to care. I grab a napkin from the pile of random things underneath my feet and start to scrub. White reveals itself as the color underneath the chalky brown side panel. The dirt shakes off into the random assortment of junk in Daniel's car.

"Petra Margaret!" she shrieks.

"Cameron Catherine Elizabeth," I parrot back. She doesn't keep going, so I look up from my shoes and find her misty-eyed. Her face is so filled with regret that I whisper, "It's okay," because I hate to see her like this. As I say it, I remember it's the same empty nothing Brooke told me just hours before.

"No." Cameron replies the same way I did. "It's really not."

"Here's an idea," Aminah says. I perk up, praying for respite. "Why don't we go inside like we planned? I'm sure we can find study guides online. And there's definitely ice cream in his freezer. And comfy clothes. I've spent twenty-four hours in a string bikini under a romper. It's time for the injustice to end."

"I second this motion," Daniel says. "Let's take a little breather before we immerse ourselves in the world of hospitals again. That lighting wounds my soul."

My eyes swell with tears again, but not for the same reason as before. Maybe my friends don't say all the things they should. And we all let secrets and problems go unnoticed for too long. But we always find a way to push away the swaying pendulum of despair. The truth is a wobble not just for me, but for everyone who hears it. When steadier ground is offered, no matter how temporary, we will always sprint toward it full speed.

······

······

Aminah packed a lot of things into my backpack. Unfortunately, the sum of those parts does not equal a full outfit, so Daniel's sleepwear fills in the gaps. It is marvelous to be out of jean shorts and in sweatpants. We pile onto his downstairs sectional, lights off, legs tossed over thighs, heads in laps, and bowls of ice cream around us. Aminah and Daniel were right. We needed a break so desperately that the relief is almost too good. Inappropriately good, considering the events that led us here. Cameron has Daniel's laptop out, scouring the internet for Honors Algebra II study guides. Daniel starts up our yearbook DVD to provide some background noise.

The menu screen is a collection of discarded yearbook photos on rotation. A girl huffing past the finish line at a track meet.

Brooke mid-dance number at a school assembly. A group of people huddled around a locker. Three guys in football uniforms kneeling in prayer. A wide shot of a parade. Two actors on stage. Daniel presses play.

Cameron puts the laptop down. Legs shift off thighs. Heads scoot from laps. Even Daniel, usually ripe for commentary and quick asides, watches in silent introspection. As each picture fades out and another pops up, I hold my breath. A crowd shot from the homecoming game appears. It's a sea of faces. So many people. So far away.

"Wait! Pause it." I fall inside the frozen image on the screen. There he is: far corner of the picture, in profile. Just the right side of his face. Undamaged. The TV screen is so large that the image distorts as I get closer.

Martin becomes pixels. Then he becomes nothing.

"Sorry," Daniel says. "I hit Stop on accident."

······

······

"What's going to happen to him?" Cameron asks.

"I've heard stories of people coming back from this before," Aminah offers.

"Me too," Daniel adds.

Cameron nods. "It's very possible."

Martin has become a kind of mythical entity. Untouchable.

Impossible. Every new piece of the puzzle only elevates his presence in my life. It's spiraling me into madness. I can hear it in my friends' voices. The way they're coddling me, as if I'm fragile. As if I need this miracle to be realized. "I'm going to lie down for a bit," I tell them.

They can think what they want. I've had a long day.

I need to see Martin.

27

There you are," Ms. Hornsby says when Petra walks into the classroom.

The overhead lights buzz like a thousand flies caught inside a jar. The room is sterile and small, without posters or desks. It is a box with a teacher and a test. Drawn blinds and forgotten memories. A clock that ticks down wasted seconds with piercing clicks.

Petra rubs her palms against her legs. The sweat won't cool. Her hands stay moist, and the lights stay unrelenting, exposing her to this moment with such unflappability that no shadow dare cross her.

Ms. Hornsby hands over the Honors Algebra II exam and promptly disappears, leaving Petra without a place to sit or a pencil to use. Panic, like a dry storm of heat and sand, rises up inside her, gritty and sharp and incapable of being tamped down by desperate swallows of saliva. The entire test seems to be written in a different language.

She looks around for something: a pencil, a person, a way out. There is nothing but the clock on the wall and the blinds over the window. There isn't even a door. She goes to the window and peeks through the horizontal slats. Outside, beyond the thick pane of glass, Martin stands atop a grassy knoll. He is distant and small. Unreachable. Petra alternates between pounding on the glass and waving her arms. She shouts his name over and over. He does not look to her.

"Martin!" she screams, willing herself to be loud enough to be heard. "I wanted to see you! To talk to you!"

She watches him hear her, the way his breath stops then speeds up, like an engine revving for a big push. She keeps screaming and pounding, and when he looks, the glass changes. It becomes the window of Ryan Hales's Jeep.

They're parked outside her house, and she's got three minutes before curfew. Something isn't right. Ryan's not right.

"I need to get inside," Petra says, looking to where she knows her house should be and only seeing Martin standing on that hill, staring at her.

Ryan unbuckles his seat belt and leans across the way. His breath is hot on Petra's cheek. "You have six minutes," he says. He's lying.

"This isn't the place," she tells him. She blinks.

Martin disappears.

It's just darkness beyond the window now. Pitch black and infinite.

Ryan moves fast, bumping into the gear shift as he heaves himself atop Petra. She scoots left and right, up and down, trying to wiggle out. But he's too heavy.

"No place is ever the place," he says before kissing her neck. He tucks a leg underneath hers, securing his pin. "This is as good as any."

"Not now."

"It's never going to be perfect, Petra." He kisses her hard.

She holds her breath. "Please stop."

He puts his hand where he shouldn't, and he's clawing around, ripping fabric, trying to do two things at once. He's got his other hand over her mouth. "*Shut up, shut up, shut up,*" he begs her.

Petra bites down on the flesh of his palm as hard as she can.

He screams out in pain, scrambling off.

She bolts out of the car. It's a full sail jump to the ground from the height of the passenger seat. A new feeling floods her. Freedom. What it smells like, sounds like, tastes like. Calm and chaos intersecting. Bitterness and relief. The worst headache of your life at the best party you've ever attended.

"You're such a dumb bitch," Ryan calls out after her. "Useless and dumb."

Words stick on her. They have real weight. They are soundtracks that score her every move. His last words tattoo onto her every thought. She's running now, but there is no destination. No matter how fast she tries to go, she makes no ground.

28

No. I had a dream, but it turned into a nightmare. The same nightmare I've had for a year straight.

That's not how this is supposed to work.

It's supposed to go like this. I fall asleep. Martin appears. We talk, and everything's better. I wake up with a swell in my chest. For a moment, I believe it's all real. The high wears off, and I take from the dream any vital information that applies to the real world. But I went back to before, when my dreams meant nothing outside of reminding me what happened last year.

Just when I think I'm getting my head above water, I go back to drowning. Sinking to the bottom of the ocean. The anchor, fixed around my legs and heavy as concrete, is Ryan Hales. His positioning—head below my thighs, arms gripped around my kneecaps—prevents me from so much as a kick. I flail my arms to no avail, rapidly descending but looking up, watching as the world above me slips away.

When will he ever leave me alone? When will I ever stop remembering?

Cameron appears. "You all right?" she asks.

"I'm fine."

"We made some food. And coffee." She nestles onto the corner of Daniel's mattress, expectant. Her eyes have a familiar redness. It's the look of complete exhaustion she wore all junior year, through the slog of ACTs and SATs and APs and every other random assortment of letters meaning too much in the moment and not enough afterward.

"It didn't work. I didn't get to talk to Martin," I tell her, needing her to be as crushed as I am. Wanting her to rip off her Art Garfunkel shirt and surrender hope.

"Skip the coffee then," she says, tucking her hands underneath my armpits to lift me up and drag me down to the kitchen. For both her benefit and mine, I lean into her.

"You just missed my parents," Daniel says as we appear, eyes as red as Cameron's. "They send their love."

"What time is it?" We've done so much today, and the sunlight still won't relent. "I had to have slept for a few hours."

Daniel places an omelet in front of me. "It's time for second breakfast." The plate is garnished with flower petals from the garden.

"It has to be later than that."

"It's never too late for breakfast."

"Thanks." I slice through my eggs, preparing to make

absentminded conversation, disappointment still stirring in my head. "Heard anything?"

Aminah turns from the couch to look at Daniel. Daniel looks at Cameron. Cameron looks at me. "You should finish your food."

"Do you want any coffee?"

"What is it?"

"Toast should be up in—"

"What is it?"

The three of them stalk me like I'm prey.

"The other car," Aminah starts.

"Don't," Cameron interrupts.

"If not now, when?"

"The driver died," Cameron says quickly.

They wait for my reaction, but I don't have one. I don't know what to do, who to be, what's appropriate.

"We saw it on the news after you went upstairs to nap," Cameron continues. "Daniel randomly turned the TV on. It's the top story right now."

Aminah rewinds the DVR for me. The voices of familiar newscasters drone on, hitting all the details I already know but speaking them with a clarity and perspective that makes my heart still. Two high school seniors taking a joy ride post graduation, alcohol in their system—Spencer above .08—blowing a red light and colliding with a man on his way back from the grocery store. Spencer's senior picture is juxtaposed against the man, a retired widower who neighbors described as "friendly but quiet." They use a photo of Martin from prom in that white tux with the orange vest. I recognize Brooke's dark hair in the corner of the frame, her face cropped out. The newscaster says Martin's in critical condition. And that's that.

I've been neglecting my phone all weekend. I've missed this news as a result. Twitter is lit up with opinions. Most people don't have kind things to say about Spencer. And why would they? What he did—

And Martin—

It's all too much.

I head back up the stairs, my eyes on my feet as they drag forward, each step heavier than the last.

29

A waltz, lilting and slow, booms from overhead speakers. Paired up in twos on a parquet floor in the middle of Petra's living room, people dance along in synchronicity. Everyone wears masks. Most are gold with long, pointed noses. Some are silver and fitted to the face. Petra, in a mask of the latter fashion and an ornate lavender ball gown that tapers in at the waist then flairs out in dramatic fashion, dances her own flowing waltz, weaving in and out of the pairs, exhilarated by the mystery of it all. She is the only one without a partner.

A man abandons his companion to grab Petra. She does not stop dancing, not even for this rude interruption, and the music accelerates with her actions, building to a feverish tempo. The man has no choice but to accompany her, and though Petra does not need a partner, she allows it, so long as she has the lead. As she pivots the man, he uses his free hand to tug on the long snout of his mask. It can't be removed.

"It's me," he says.

Petra doesn't react. The man claws at his mask again, but it will not budge. Instead it changes, the long nose growing into autumn leaves.

"Who are you?" Petra asks, twirling the man with the morphing mask, feigning amusement.

He yanks on the leafy branch representing his nose, desperate to remove it. "Martin!" he cries. His mask morphs again, turning blue, almost melting into his skin.

Petra spins him in a constant, cruel circle. "You see, I'm having too much fun to be bothered by you," she says. She speaks like she's older than she is. Wiser and less afraid.

The man grabs her shoulders, trying to make his eyes meet hers. He digs his heels into the ground to stop the whirling.

"Fine," Petra says. "But I already told your friend about your letter."

The violins reach a shattering crescendo. The floor vibrates. Dancing pairs make frenzied figure eights around Petra and the masked man, who she knows to be Martin, though it isn't a Martin she wants to know anymore.

"I know you did," he says. His mask changes again, becoming almost animalistic, made of rotting flesh from unknown sources, looking less like a mask and more like excess skin on a feral beast. "Thank you."

The ceiling disappears. A bolt of lightning strikes the floor between where the two stand.

"I didn't know how to help you in your last dream, and then I disappeared," he tells her.

The dancers around them continue. The quality of their movement sours with the music. Everything is minor chords and dissonance. Disjointed, ever-changing tempos. Rain begins to pour down.

"What do you mean?" she asks, feigning innocence.

"In your other dream. With that guy in the car. I wasn't thinking right. I was trying to become nothingness to see if that would make me wake up."

She turns from him. "I don't need you to help me. I do fine on my own."

"No, I know." He shakes his head, rubbing his hands where his temples would be if there wasn't a mask covering his face. "I didn't mean it to come off like that. I don't know what was going on, but the part I saw before I left didn't look good." He pauses. "I meant I'm sorry that happened."

"It's none of your business."

"No, it isn't. But if something happened to you, I'm still upset."

She picks up her heavy skirt and runs. Her house no longer has any doors. It is one endless, ceilingless living room, the parquet floor expands, building to follow her every step. Unable to hold her dress up and run at the same time, she stumbles and falls, helplessly, soundlessly.

Martin catches up. The powerful spray of rain has made his mask more heinous. He looks like a creature risen from deep beneath the ground.

"Don't touch me!" Petra tries to say, but it's as if she's only mouthing it. The chaos is too loud. "Leave me alone!"

"I don't want to hurt you," he tells her, and he means it. "I'm scared too. They say you shouldn't fight quicksand, but then how do you escape? I'm running out of ideas." He crumples. "I need help."

Petra considers relenting. He's understood her, even when she can't be heard. She thinks better of it and continues cowering.

Martin is careful not to touch any part of her, even the trim of her puffed gown. "I'm stuck between living and dying. That's what I've been trying to say to you all this time."

"I already know that," Petra says. Her head is buried in her arm, and the rain sneaks around her hair to form a puddle in the basin created from her elbow and forearm. "There are brain bleeds. We don't know how bad it is." The water tickles her nose as she speaks. She quite likes the feeling of the cool refreshing wetness underneath her own mask. It makes her feel safe. Close. Protected from the monster on Martin's face.

"How long has it been since the accident?" Martin asks.

"Three days," Petra tells him.

"That's it? It's been forever for me." He gets quieter. "Please help. I don't know what to do anymore."

His words devastate her. Doesn't he know how much she's been trying? What more can she do? Rising from her puddle to face him, she focuses only the edges of his mask, where his normal skin is visible underneath. "Why did you do that?" she cries out. "Why did you leave early? What were you thinking?" With one hand on either corner, her fingers wrap around the mask. She tugs hard, putting all her weight into it. The force of the motion takes her to the ground. "People are dead!" she cries out. "People are *dead*! Why did you do that?"

In her hands, the mask changes again. It becomes the face of Ryan Hales, mangled and battered, but still moving. She looks back to the body beside her. A gaping, bloody wound is where the face should be, and the body reaches out desperately, arms like fishes flopping out of water.

Petra screams: two short yells then one long wail, like a flatlining heart monitor.

30

I hear two short yells then one long wail, like a flatlining heart monitor.

It's me. I'm screaming.

But not aloud.

I'm screaming in my mind.

I shoot up from Daniel's bed, panting, covered in sweat. My hands fumble for the bedside lamp. A warm glow lights up the black sheets and casts shadows on the wall it's closest to, but in the corners, where a soft breeze from the open window makes waves with the curtains, darkness still lurks. I need that air to wake me up. Shake my nightmare's hold on me. I open Daniel's closet door and throw one of his hoodies on over his track T-shirt. Head covered by the hood, I tiptoe down the stairs, past Aminah and Cameron asleep on the sectional and Daniel on the chaise, over to my shoes. One shoe on, the other in my hand, I hop out the front door and into the still world of nighttime suburbia, triggering the motion-censored porch lamp. It casts a spotlight on me. I scurry onto the sidewalk.

The night above is clear and confident. I set my pace to match it. As I move into the breeze, it cools the sweat slicked onto my skin. I walk streetlamp to streetlamp, crossing empty intersections and past red lights. It doesn't take long for my body to go numb, a helpless soldier to my thoughts, carrying me to the only place that makes sense right now. The beginning and the end of all of this madness.

There's an opening in the chain link fence that surrounds the football field. I slip through as I've seen countless others do, sneaking into and out of class. Just as Ryan once did to catch me walking out of school. *Hey! Petra, right?*

The field is vast. No gym classes. No Friday night game lights. No white plastic chairs lined up in endless rows.

Just me.

......

Petra took me to a masquerade straight out of a movie I'd never admit to enjoying. A mask was on my face that I couldn't take off, and Petra didn't seem to want to believe that I was me. It was like I hurt her somehow, sometime between the hill dream and this one.

My doing nothing was definitely not helpful. Another bad idea from Martin McGee.

Rocking back and forth with my arms around a girl's waist. I have that down cold. But talking to Petra meant real dancing.

Lots of spinning around and carefully timed steps. I was better than I've ever been in life, that's for sure, but it was still hard. We swayed and swirled, and she spoke like she was older. The mask on my face wouldn't come off. Instead, it kept changing.

She was scared of me.

I was scared of me.

Who the hell am I anymore?

Saying I was stuck between living and dying was old news to her. Everyone in the real world knows way more about me than I do. And she said it's been only three days. Three freakin' days.

It's been a century for me.

Still I asked for help, and man, do I love that glowing girl, because she got up and wrapped her hands around the edges of my mask. She pulled back so hard she fell. I felt a pain completely different than the accident. Not bones crushing, but like, my entire personhood going away. I was trapped in a faceless body, reaching for her. She was yelling at me. *Why did you do that? Why did you leave? People are dead!*

People are dead?

What does that mean?

Every time I think I understand, it becomes clear to me that I don't know a thing. These questions multiply. This place is a vacuum, sucking me up then shooting me back out, leaving nothing clean.

......

I lie down on the fifty-yard line. Right in the middle. The grass is cold and dewy. It leaks in through my hoodie, the cotton flirting with the dampness, making my back feel prickly and warm all the same, like it's a towel wrapped around me after a long swim. The sky is an impossible distance away from where I am. There is space for entire life spans between us. So much spare room for every ugly thing tumbling around inside of me. Masquerades with Martin and Ryan. Collided. Colliding. My mind tangling the two of them up in a battle for my attention.

For a while, I convinced myself that I loved Ryan. The idea of him at least. The way his presence broke up my routine. How everyone's eyes opened wider on me, wondering how love would change me, watching close as I pretended to care more about another person than I did about myself. It's a rite of passage to have your heart broken in high school, and I wanted that award like I wanted all the rest. But it didn't work out quite right. Just like the rest. It was the wrong guy at the wrong time. The wrong intentions steering me down the wrong course, ending with his right hand over my mouth. His left between my legs. Up too high. Fingers moving. Pressing. Fighting. Too much. Too soon. The flesh of his palm clamped around my teeth.

I thought I knew, but I knew nothing.

I'm sick, Mom. I can't go to my final today.

The voicemail he left me the night before graduation. "I'm back in town. Just let me talk to you."

His calls streaming in between my parents and my sisters: an insistent, steady pest, always buzzing right outside my ear, never swatted away.

I wasn't ready to talk a year ago. I'm still not ready now. I don't know if I'll ever be.

He doesn't have a right to be here, written into the pain on my face, holding on to the tear falling down my cheek, resting as a hulking anchor at the pit of my stomach, but he is all the same.

A part of me wants to tear into him with my every spiteful word. Break his spine through the sheer force of my verbal tirade.

Another part of me wants to bleach every trace of his existence.

Beneath my skin and all my organs, in the place where instinct lives, a core that has no place in medical books, no identifiable source, I feel this conflict with such immensity that it goes into territory that can never be mapped. There is so much, too much, power in the unknown.

It is boundaries crossed. Apologies unsaid. Explanations not given.

It is night. It is secrets.

It is Martin and me singing songs in this very spot. Nudging elbows. Stealing laughs. Hammering into the well of possibility with the first hesitant clinks, unsure of how much there is to mine from such a new, delicate source. All I haven't gotten the chance to know about him infects my bloodstream. He could be someone to me.

The complete, devastating, tantalizing unknown.

But someone is dead because of that car crash. Some man whose life story never before intersected with mine. Someone who had dreams and nightmares and fears and joys. A full person with a full world I'll never know. It doesn't seem right or fair, yet I cannot blink it away. It is not my nightmare. It's my reality.

Maybe fairness is nothing but an idea we've made up. Maybe we've all tricked ourselves into believing kindness equals fairness, when really kindness masks the truth of things, and fairness doesn't have a moral compass. Why didn't I tell my friends what Ryan did? I thought, *That's not fair to put that on them*, but no, it was kindness, a courtesy. Don't wear this burden with me. Go on thinking that we're all fine. We must keep soldiering on. We must survive high school.

And they did. They made it to the top of the mountain, as Cameron says. But I got lost last year, and I never recovered. Now I'm tumbling back down, falling farther away from the peak I was supposed to reach on Friday afternoon, slamming into every rock I sidestepped on the way up. Ryan Hales is still in my head, continuing to distract me from the things I should be doing.

My last chance at this final is hours away. One more shard of the glass he shattered inside of me, waiting to be swept up. And I don't know if I can. Because of him. Again.

And Martin.

He keeps asking me to help him. This I want to do—it's all I've been doing the past few days—but I'm not a doctor. I'm not a psychic. I am just a girl who dreams so big that other people can climb inside and take refuge. I don't know why it's me, but I know it matters. Maybe it started as a way to avoid my problems, but it's so much bigger now. It is the size of the space between the sky and me.

I cannot fight fairness. I cannot fight death. The only thing I can fight is myself. Stop my fears from clouding my dreams.

Steal the last remnants of Ryan's power over me and use it to give Martin a moment like the one I'm in now, my back on the wet grass of the fifty-yard line, small stars peeking through the blackness like secrets the night reveals only for me. Not running from or falling into anything. Not right now, at least. Tomorrow. Always tomorrow. But not now. In this moment, in the dark of the complete unknown, nothing can hurt me.

I breathe in. I breathe out.

At least I am alive.

31

The masquerade has been restored to its original state: opulent and joyous. Petra places herself back into the action. Her dress is now simpler. A sleek silhouette, black and fitted, seams tickling the edge of the parquet. Her long hair flows loose. The ringlets turn inward to frame her face. She wears no mask.

Martin, she thinks over and over, his name her only internal monologue. She wants Martin here. He appears in a well-tailored tuxedo with hair to match the part, slicked down and to the side. No mask either.

"What happened?" he asks as Petra pulls herself into him. The two begin to dance to an internal beat. Their slow, close rhythm does not match the cotton candy dancers around them, so Petra wishes them away. Her living room becomes the empty football field cloaked by star-speckled night.

"I'm sorry," she says, "I keep letting fear win."

The two step side to side, forward and backward, always in harmony.

Martin sucks in air. "That's not true at all," he tells her. "I think you keep beating fear."

Petra rests her head on his shoulder. They continue to move to the beat of their secret song.

"What did you mean when you said people are dead?" Martin asks.

Petra places her finger on his lips to shush him. "Not now." Her hands wrap back around Martin's neck. "Be patient," she says. "Just exist with me."

Martin holds tighter to her waist. "Existing is goddamn underrated," he says back.

The countless stars above blanket them, making everything soft and safe. In the dark of the complete unknown, nothing can hurt either of them.

They are alive.

And for now, that is enough.

PART FOUR

32

I t is the last day of high school, the sun is shining, the newly
tuned Caravan's driving smoother than ever, and all Fly
can think about is some girl he sat next to at graduation?
Congratulations! Let me pull over and buy you a trophy, Spencer
thinks to himself. He presses his foot into the gas pedal. *This
is flying, Fly. Earn your nickname.* When he looks to see Fly's
reaction, he finds Fly reaching for the steering wheel.

There is a dot on the scenery beyond the passenger window.
A piece of dirt that keeps getting bigger, trying to erase everything in sight.

Oh.

It's a car.

"Fly, look out! Look out!" Spencer yells. He slams on the brakes.

Fly tugs the steering wheel to the left.

The car smashes into the passenger side of the White Whale,

halfway between the front seat and the back seat. Forward and sideways forces combine to slam Spencer into the airbag and door. As his head collides with the heavy pillow of the bag and the glass of the window, breaking his nose and jumbling his brain, he can find only one thought.

I might've *killed my best friend.*

Because Fly swerved the wheel.

Once the car finally stops shoving the Caravan away, Spencer breathes again. He can't seem to use his nose, so it's a desperate gasp through his mouth. Unbridled sobs release from deep inside of him. He looks over to see what's happened to Fly: his aggravating, annoying, frustrating best friend in the entire universe.

The seat belt keeps Fly's body upright, and the airbag has his head propped up at an awkward angle. Spencer unbuckles and leans over the gears to try and hold together body parts that seem to be falling off. He screams out as many swear words as he can come up with, none of which seem to capture what it is to be holding his dying friend in his arms.

Fly coughs. His eyes flicker open.

Spencer stops cursing. "Fly?" No response. "Marty?"

The body goes limp in Spencer's arms once again.

33

MONDAY, JUNE 11

If I live or if I die or if I'm forever in this Between, the people I love are still hurting. Apologizing into thin air certainly didn't do a thing to change that. Doing nothing did, well, nothing. Big surprise. Asking for help doesn't make much sense. No one can get me out of a place they've never been themselves.

Small changes. That's what it is. The loop Spits is caught in must be changed until it's fixed, no matter what it means for me. Spitty needs to move on. It's not all his fault.

It's mine too.

......

Flat on my back, Daniel's hoodie soaked by dew and freezing my skin, I can only half remember how I arrived here. It started with a nightmare and a need for air. Now the light of a new day lifts the veil off the sleeping world, and I'm lying in the middle of the football field. I've woken up in some odd places this weekend, but none stranger than here.

......

Petra pulled me back to the masquerade, but this time without all the bad things. It was just her and me dancing, alone on the football field, dressed in our finest. Her dream lasted for its own eternity, then faded out like a movie you could watch over and over, letting it play all the way through the end credits. The beauty of the way she looked, the way we moved together, the quiet of the night—it was exactly what I needed to know I'm not alone.

......

It's coming back to me. Martin and I dancing on the football field, dressed in our finest. He kept asking questions, but I didn't answer. I asked him to exist with me. Be patient for once. He listened. He let me dance with him.

I clutch my chest, pulling the perfect night in close. Whenever I need to, I can transport myself back to the star-covered football field, rest my head on Martin's shoulder, and let the warmth of the memory lift my feet off the ground.

......

Petra asked me to be patient. I reminded myself of that as I came back to the scene of the accident. Being patient there meant putting up with the pain of pushing against the invisible fortress of Spitty's memory. Knowing that moving the steering wheel wouldn't be enough, but it would be a start. Small changes.

I almost stopped it all from happening.

Almost.

......

With a thud, I come crashing down. Someone is dead.

Then panic shoots through every vertebra of my spine. It's Monday.

The exam is today.

......

It might be a coincidence, or it might be a result of the small change, but things are shifting again, like they did the first time I died. If I squeeze my eyes, which seem to somehow be back in the head I sort of have again, there is something like sound. White noise. I'm not remembering it. I'm hearing it, like it's really there.

It should scare me, but it doesn't. I have a safe place. A mind I can trust, even when everything turns to chaos. Someone who can find me when I think I might be lost forever.

I have Petra.

34

Slipping in as I slipped out, I find everything the way I left it. I've felt an overwhelming sense of nausea since I left the school. Among many other things, I remembered that I left Daniel's door unlocked and I didn't bring my cell phone. Seeing the peaceful sleeping faces of my three best friends helps settle my nerves a bit. The little night trip was just for me, and I'm the only one who will ever know. I tiptoe up the staircase and back into Daniel's room. My cell phone sits on the nightstand beside Daniel's bed. I grab it to check the time.

It's still so early. I have hours before I need to be at the school for my final.

I clear out all my voicemails so that I never have to listen to my parents' pleading messages or Ryan's incessant begging for a chance to talk. Feeling emboldened, I send him my own message.

I owe you nothing. I don't have to speak to you if I don't want to. And I don't want to. There's nothing more to say than that. Please leave me alone. Goodbye.

I block his number.

It's so simple, yet so powerful. One small step toward a bigger change.

I glance at the rest of my unread texts and notice one from my sister Jessica.

I'm sorry that I didn't tell M&D where you were. Mom said Dad threatened to kick you out and then you actually left. When I got home last night, Dad was crying in the kitchen. It was the weirdest thing. I don't know if that helps, but I know he feels bad. We all do. Please come home. Or call me. You could call Caroline too I guess, but we all know I'm your favoritest sister ;) I love you, Petty. And I'm sooo proud of you! Eleventh in the class is only two lower than my rank. Screw Caroline and her valedictorian crown! Haha! But really, a little secret. In college, none of what you did in high school will matter.

My parents still haven't told my sisters about the whole not officially graduating thing. Maybe they'll never have to. That would be nice.

I take a shower.

With a towel wrapped around my head and not a stitch of makeup on my face, I throw on whatever clothes I can scrounge together. I can't believe it was only three days ago I stood in front of my mirror getting ready for Martin's party, making sure my makeup portrayed my casual coolness and my hair showed my effort without screaming it. Now I'm grateful Aminah grabbed clean underwear.

Back in the bedroom, Daniel's covers wear my impression, waiting for me to fill the crinkled outline in with my weight. I oblige. My new clothes are a little damp from my hair dripping out from beneath my towel. The cool water on the warm pillow creates a perfect contrast.

I set an alarm on my phone.

I close my eyes.

One last moment of peace.

35

The soft pulse of distant music comes through first. The crunch of people eating chips and the shuffling of feet follow. Indecipherable pieces of conversations start floating by—chattering, static, like a TV that's been left on without being turned to a proper channel. It's all a restrained kind of loud. Sound that doesn't carry far outside of itself.

Petra's perspective sharpens. Now, she can smell detergent and cigarettes in the air, and she can see she's in a basement she doesn't know. At the same time, it's the kind of place she knows well: a stock suburban hangout of the well-used variety. The ceiling is too low, and the carpet is worn thin, making obvious the poured concrete beneath it. In the center of the room, there is a gigantic beige sectional. It's tufted and pillowy and designed for naps and for going days without seeing sunlight. The flat-screen TV in front of it is bigger than a TV has any right to be. There are two Mario Kart points of view on its screen. Petra looks from the game back to the couch and realizes Turrey and Spencer are on the sectional, side by side, remotes in hand. Their focus is impressive. The game rules them.

The other kids in the room are scattered about, talking and laughing and eating chips. A warm feeling floods Petra. It's knowing that for this night, the dark will never be too dark. The late will never feel too late. It will just transform into early morning, which is even better. Because this is Martin's party.

She finally made it.

Finding him isn't hard. He's in the back of the room, leaning into the space between walls, looking at Petra. She wants to meet him where he stands, but her legs are incapable of moving. The last time she saw him, they were dancing on the football field.

Things feel different now. They're…more.

"This your idea of a party?" Martin calls out. He grins like he's teasing her. "Everyone's eating chips and drinking water."

If she could, she'd breathe a sigh of relief. He always makes things feel easy. "Considering the events of the past week, I think they're all being more than reasonable." It's awkward bringing it up, but it has to be said.

"I like that you expect the best from people!" Martin shouts. There's no reason to be as loud as he is, but it helps lessen the tension all the same. He knows how to pivot a conversation. He also seems to know Petra can't bring herself to move toward him, so he comes to join her in the open space between the back of his couch and the wall where he'd been standing.

"Shouldn't we all expect the best from people?"

Across from her and Martin, next to the stairs, there's an old pool table. It's covered in folded laundry and random boxes, save for the center, which has been cleared out. In the open space, Cameron, Aminah, Daniel, and Brooke sit cross-legged in a circle of sorts, playing hot hands. Petra smiles at the sight of them. They look so happy.

"I'm impressed. This is almost exactly what my basement really looks like," Martin says, pulling her attention back to him. "Our couch isn't that big, but other than that, you've got it down. It even smells right. Like soap and stale tobacco." He pauses to marvel. "I wouldn't have known how to explain that before. With all my time away, I can really smell it now."

Petra blushes. "I was in your house the other day. I didn't see the basement, but I could figure out how it would be."

"You were in my house?"

"Yeah. When we were looking for your letter."

"Oh." He sits down and folds his legs. He looks so young, hands resting in his lap, legs crossed. "A lot of life has happened since my accident, huh?"

She'd been so mad at him yesterday. She still is now. What he did was beyond reckless. Ignorant. Neglectful. There is no excusing it. Yet none of it matches up with the boy she knows in her dreams. Why didn't he stop Spitty from drinking and driving? Someone is *dead*. She shudders at the thought.

Martin cocks his head to take in her reaction.

The battle between her anger and her sentimentality has to

be settled, if temporarily. Martin's life is too fragile right now. She joins him on the ground. "Nothing you can't catch up on," she says. Fighting is a bridge better crossed in person. He has to make it out of this alive first. Then she can yell. Oh, how she will yell.

Martin takes inventory of his friends scattered about the party. "That's true. We seem to run with the same crowd these days."

"You know good people."

Martin points to Spencer, who is currently leaning into Turrey so that Turrey can't see the game on the screen. "Even Spits?"

"To be honest, I don't know why he's here," Petra admits. "I don't have full control over all of this. Some of the people at this party are my best friends, and then some are members of my old Girl Scout troop. A couple of people from random extracurriculars I've done over the years. Some people I've never seen before in my life." She points to a girl sitting on the coffee table, staring at her phone. "But that's my sister Jessica's best friend from day care. There's a picture of her and Jess on our fridge. It's like nineteen years old at this point. I couldn't even tell you that girl's name. No idea how she made the cut."

They laugh. It's all so absurd, yet somehow, right now, it makes perfect sense.

It occurs to her then that there's one person who hasn't snuck into the party. One person who's chased her for a full year.

But not tonight.

She smiles to herself. Small victories.

"Let's try something." Martin stands up. "If I tell you what I was planning on wearing to this actual party, maybe you can make it so that I *am* wearing it. Because I've got to say, this look isn't cutting it." He's in a hospital gown.

How had she not noticed? Maybe he wasn't before. The rules are blurry. Everything is on a constant tilt, forever shifting into different focuses.

"I was gonna find my dad's old Van Halen shirt for you," Martin continues. "I know he has one lying around somewhere. It's the one with a smoking angel baby on it. Do you know it?"

"Kind of." She tries to conjure the image, and it appears on Martin, along with a pair of well-fitted blue jeans.

Martin looks down and cheers. "Petty Margs for the win!" He considers the look. "I'd have topped this off with my usual Cubs hat though."

She gives him the hat.

He takes it off his head to examine it. "Whoa. This is pretty damn close to correct. You're *good.*" He pauses. "One more thing. Some Nikes on my feet?"

"Okay, I'm not your personal stylist here. Plain socks will have to do."

"Can't have it all," Martin says with a grin.

"Shouldn't we be trying to teleport or fly or something?"

Martin sits back down. Their knees are touching now. "I don't know about you, but I'm a simple person. I don't need much more than what's in this room right now. Maybe my family. That'd be nice."

Petra thinks of them, and they appear: Mama Dorothy, Mr. McGee, Katie, and her husband Rick. They walk through the door, laughing. Katie carries a cake with a lit candle. "Congratulations, graduate!" she cheers.

The entire party focuses on Martin as Katie brings him the cake. It reads CONGRATS, MARTY in blue icing. A little frosting Cubs hat is over the M.

The whole room erupts in applause. "Fly! Fly! Fly!" they chant.

Martin stands to look at the candle. He makes a wish, and a puff of smoke clouds his face, making the room smell like a birthday. Like hope.

Mama Dorothy kisses Martin on the cheek and squeezes him. His dad gets in on the other side. While his parents hold him, Katie carries the cake over to the pool table. Plates and forks and napkins are there now. She starts cutting off a big piece. Just as Mama Dorothy and Mr. McGee let go of Martin, Katie takes the chunk of cake she's cut and smashes it into his face.

"Love you, dummy," she says. She gives him a hug. They're both laughing hysterically.

Martin licks his lips. "Yeah. Love you too, loser."

Rick waits behind her with a napkin. He hands it off to Martin once Katie lets him go.

"Always lookin' out for me, Ricky," Martin says as he wipes his face clean. Rick pats him on the back.

The family moves toward the pool table again. Mama Dorothy and Katie start cutting the cake up for the guests to enjoy. Jessica's friend from day care is first to get to them, almost aggressive in her eagerness. The rest of the party forms a line behind her. It's so pure, all these teenagers waiting for a slice of cake, Mama Dorothy and Katie diligently obliging, cutting squares and passing them out as fast as they can.

Only Petra and Martin are left behind.

"Don't you dare ask what I wished for," Martin jokes. His delivery lacks the usual sparkle. Tears are in his eyes.

"I know better than that."

There's a lot they aren't saying. It's too hard to speak about.

Martin closes the distance between them, pulling Petra in for a hug. It's tight and personal, but it isn't romantic. It's more— sentimental maybe. It makes her want to cry. He's right here, hugging her so tight she almost can't breathe, and she misses him. She misses all the time they didn't know each other. All the days she didn't turn her head to the side or look around the lunch-room. How many times did she see him and not notice?

How many times did he see her?

She buries her head into his shoulder, trying to flatten out the aching feeling that's ballooning inside her. He matches her for a moment, then lessens his grip. "I better go cross something off my checklist," he says as he breaks the hug.

It's good that he did it. She wasn't sure she'd ever let go.

"What?" She doesn't know where he's going with this.

"C'mon, Petra. I can't believe you don't remember our first conversation. *It's like I don't even know you anymore.*" He pretends to sound scorned. The tears that once filled his eyes have already fallen, tracing lines down his cheek. "I can't check off 'watch *Back to the Future,*' because we haven't watched it yet, but—"

Petra recalls the list he made:

1. Watch *Back to the Future*
2. Look in the yearbook
3. Understand what there is to love about this place.

He doesn't say the third list item, but he quirks his face. His sentence stays unfinished. Petra hears it all the same.

"I'm sorry I've failed you," she whispers.

Now he's the one that doesn't understand.

"I can't figure out how to bring you back," she finishes.

He checks around her neck for something. "Nope. Not here." He continues looking, peeking in the pocket on her shirt, turning her from side to side. "Not here either."

"What are you doing?"

"Checking for a stethoscope. Maybe a lab coat folded up into your pocket. Or one of those little prescription pads. Anything that would show me you're a doctor. Because if you aren't, I'm pretty sure you can't *actually* bring me back."

She almost rolls her eyes at him. Their conversations never hit true endings, just pauses. There's always something more to talk about. "You keep asking me for help. And I'm not helping."

Martin puts his hands on her shoulders. He locks eyes with her, staring with such intention that she'd never dare look away. "If you can only remember one thing about this dream when you wake up, I need it to be this." He pauses, considering something. "Fair warning, I'm gonna go full cheesy because that's the kind of guy I am. Okay? Stick with me." He secures his stance. "You aren't failing. Not at all. In fact, you helped me figure out something really important. You know how everybody says everything happens for a reason? I realized that's not what it is. It's that you have to make a good reason out of everything that happens. That's the only control we have." He lets her go. "You helped me know I'm never alone, even when I'm feeling pretty goddamn alone."

Petra's crying now. She can't help it. "You listen to me too," she says as she wipes tears from her cheeks. "You better be patient. We're gonna get you to wake up."

He sticks his pinkie out. "Deal?"

She locks her pinkie in his. "Deal."

Another pact is made.

36

When I creep out of the bedroom after my alarm goes off, I see that Cameron, Aminah, and Daniel are awake, watching me descend the stairs. I feel like the main character of a movie in which I never asked to star. It's the way their eyes track my every movement, expecting something important from me.

"Morning," I say. "Hope you guys slept well."

Aminah's nursing a black coffee. "I was out cold. I haven't slept like that since I was a kid."

"Proud of you. You made it all the way to nine a.m." I get a bigger laugh than I deserve.

"And I didn't even need to break into my house and get clothes for the day. I've got yours to wear!" Aminah says.

Daniel places a cup of coffee in front of me. "We've all done more with our time in the last three days than we did with all of high school, what with trying to save someone's life and all."

It's the wrong choice of words. It sits there, and I realize what they're waiting for this time is the breakdown they think I'm still holding in. They don't know that I've let so much of it go. To deflect, I explain that I need to leave. It's time to correct my last lingering mistake. *To make a good reason out of everything that happens.* My latest dream comes flooding back to me. With it, a surge of new confidence. I made a promise to Martin. I have to hold up my end of the deal.

"Did you study?" Cameron asks.

"Whoops! Gotta go," I say as I check an imaginary watch. I'm out the door before they can say another word.

······

I promised Petra I'd be patient. I will. I mean, I *am*. But there's all this drive in me now and nowhere to put it. I've seen glimpses of the way life's moving on without me. It's happening. Petra's friends have found my friends. A good reason is being made out of this.

What I've been missing is that it's not about getting help. It's about giving it. I was on the right track with the whole small changes thing. But now it's time to go big or go home for the one person who needs to be free more than I do.

Spits.

······

I stare down the same front doors I've entered every Monday of what seems like my entire life. I am the last senior on Earth. Maybe the universe.

Missing this final has been nothing but an excuse. A way to keep myself safe from a world I wasn't ready to understand. Avoid everything and never get hurt again. But the real world threw itself on me like paint. It covers my clothes. My thoughts. All of me. I am so much more than the white linoleum and the white brick walls and the buzzing white fluorescent lights. So much more than Ryan's Jeep and the way he hurt me. So much more than I ever gave myself credit for.

The hallways shrink as I grow taller. I swear the top of my head grazes the ceiling outside of Ms. Hornsby's classroom.

......

Paging Spitty Alan Kuspits Jr.

It's me, your best friend, Martin Frederick McGee. I'd like to have a word with you. Please allow me the opportunity to enter your dream again.

I know. You think dreams are pointless. You've never shared yours with me, except for one time—the most important time. You told me about the one where you saw your mom, and she told you everything would be okay. This is like that. Just like that.

Go to sleep. You have to be tired. Your head's hit the airbag like a million times too many now, your nose ballooning up on the spot, gushing blood. Reminds me of eighth-grade gym when Chris kicked the soccer ball at Turrey's face and tried to act like it wasn't on purpose, even though we all knew it was totally on purpose. Turrey got so much blood all over his gym shirt and Mr. Healy made him get a new one the next week because he kept rewearing the bloody one to piss off Chris. Give Turrey a back pat from me for that, will you? That was classic.

But seriously, you were messed up. I promise this is the last time I'm going to let that happen to you. Promise on the pact. Speaking of, when this is all done, I do want you to double-check my body like we promised. There's a chance I'm not understanding how all this works. I trust that you'll make sure. And give that letter to my family. It was almost ten years ago that I wrote it, so the spelling's probably pretty shoddy—I still get hung up on the word *remember*—but the idea of it is right. Be happy. Move on. Make a good reason out of everything that happens.

Spitty Kuspits, let's go for one last joy ride in the White Whale.

......

"You're early," Ms. Hornsby says as I enter her classroom. I did so many things, and I'm still ahead of schedule.

"Is that okay?"

"I'm glad you're here at all." She pulls a timer out of her drawer and hands it to me. Then she hands me a Scantron and the exam questions. All business. "Set this for fifty minutes and turn in the final when it starts beeping." She nods and returns to grading papers.

As I look at the exam on my way down the aisle, it really hits me. If I don't succeed, I'm forever trapped in a place I don't want to be anymore, giving power to a memory that doesn't deserve that kind of control over me.

My phone starts buzzing. "Oh, yes, that. I almost forgot. No phones," Ms. Hornsby says. "Bring it up here."

I pull it out of my purse and see that Turrey is calling. I stall, unsure if I should answer or hand my phone over. "Can I take this really quick?"

"It's now or never, Petra."

I miss Turrey's call. Within seconds, Cameron is calling.

Ms. Hornsby stands and walks over to me. "Whoever it is, they can wait. Your future is more important." *The phrase of the century.* She snatches the phone from my grasp and gives me a textbook teacher's glare. "Now or never."

......

You're always late, Spitty. I saw you push the other people aside to scoot down your row into your seat. I still don't understand how you were late to your own graduation and you still managed to get your parking spot. "You can't rush perfection, man." That's what you'd say about it. That's what you always say.

But I need you to hurry.

I need you to let me help.

......

The timer beeps.

It's over. I'm done. I walk up the aisle and turn in my final.

Ms. Hornsby hands me my phone in response. "You're quite popular today. This has been going off all hour."

I don't know why, but I decide to tell her the truth. "It's probably about Martin."

Color drains from her face. Gone is her signature icy facade.

She was on Martin's case the entire ceremony, but I have a sneaking suspicion she was hard on him because she liked him. She knew, like I know, that he's capable of being more. "Has there been any update? Administration's been in contact with the hospital, but we haven't heard anything in a while."

I look at the new voicemails on my phone. One from Turrey and one from Cameron, as well as several missed calls from both. And lots of unread texts. "I'm going to guess those calls were with news."

"I'm sorry I made you wait. I didn't realize you two actually knew each other." An idea comes to her. "I can run this test through the Scantron and let you know how you did if you'd like? Maybe you can listen to those voicemails while I do it. It will take only a minute or two." She squeezes my shoulder. "I'd really like to know. About both of you."

Her desperation makes me agree. And my curiosity. Maybe if I did it—accomplished the seemingly impossible—Martin can do it too.

When Ms. Hornsby leaves the classroom, I sit in a front row desk and play Turrey's voicemail.

"Hey. I just left Daniel's, and you weren't there. Mama D called me. Said the docs are saying Fly's made a turn for the worse. He's stable for now, but it's been up and down all morning. Shit. Sorry if you can't hear me. I have this on speaker 'cuz I'm driving. It's—I don't know. I felt like I had to call you. Hit me back when you can."

Then Cameron's.

"Hey, Petty. Hope the final is going well. You're gonna do great.

If anyone can pull it off without studying, it's you. I'm rambling. I'm sorry. Turrey told us something. This is…I don't know. I love you. We're driving to the school now. We'll be outside when you finish. I love you. I know I already said that. I love you."

……

Spencer, I'm not trying to rush perfection, I swear. I need it to be your dream next. It can't be Petra's.

I've been seeing her a lot here. More than I've seen anyone else, actually. If it's her before you, with her long pretty hair and her glow and her smart way of talking, she'll make me ask more questions and force me to be even more patient until another answer presents itself. This Between—with the waiting in the blink and the idea of pain and the kinda, almost, sort of body— is the closest I've come to mastering the art of patience. But it's been long enough. Helping you is an answer I like. Your life must be bonkers in the real world. This was the worst choice we've ever made in our lives, by far. They get to chew you out there. On my side, you've got to let it go. I'd rather sit in on a dream of us playing ukuleles on a beach. I'd even go to a Sox game with you. But we need to handle this crash dream, then call a truce. Okay?

Nothing is weirder than feeling like you're right under the surface of yourself, and I say this as a formerly dead kid who's spent three days climbing into people's dreams. It's like my body is the air above the pool, and I'm swimming toward it, and I know I'm about to break through, so I keep swimming, but I'm not breaking through.

So come on, Spencer.

I need it to be you next.

......

Ms. Hornsby comes back in the room, beaming. She hands me the Scantron. Seventy-four out of one hundred. The old version of me would've been mortified by that grade. This Petra is elated.

"I did it," I say, feeling the weight of the words in my mouth. Something close to a grin almost creeps onto my face, but I bite it back, thinking of Martin.

"You did," she confirms. "I'll let admin know straightaway." She sits at her desk. "How's Martin?"

I choke out the details Turrey and Cameron left me in their voicemails. So much waiting. So many unknowns.

Ms. Hornsby chews over my update. "I can't believe I'm saying this, but after he transferred out of my class, I actually missed having him as a student." She cuts her stare back over to me. "You better get down there and see him."

I give her a hug. "Thank you, Ms. Hornsby."

My gesture surprises her. She tenses up then surrenders to it. Once we break apart, she gives me this wise, all-knowing look. "Now that I'm officially not your teacher anymore, I can tell you what I know. You're not the type of person who takes anything lightly. Whatever made you avoid this test was something big. I'm proud of you for coming here and doing it. I wish your grade was higher, but hey, I wouldn't be a good math teacher if I said I was happy with a C."

She gives me a significant look that I'm not sure how to decipher.

"If you ever need to talk, I'm here," she says, as if to explain. "I'm sorry I didn't tell you that earlier. I wanted you to learn a lesson. I'm big enough to admit that I could have handled it better. We all could have. We could see there was a real problem, and our solution wasn't the best." She leans forward to whisper. "I'll tell you another secret. We teachers are still learning too."

It's incredible the power in having even one adult let me know she saw me struggling, and she handled it wrong too. Not just me. I spent my whole academic life crafting the image that I was willing to do whatever it took for my grades, most nights choosing studying over sleep, the rings under my eyes like badges of honor. You do it long enough, and eventually everyone accepts that it's worth it to ignore your humanity in pursuit of helping you be the *best*. Then something real happens to you, and no one knows what to do. They treat you like a malfunctioning machine. That's how I treated myself too. I was assaulted, and I let myself believe it meant I was broken.

I'm not.

"I really appreciate you saying that," I tell Ms. Hornsby. "And thank you for working with the school to give me so many chances. I know it's more than most people get. I hope you realize that every kid who's struggling probably has a reason and deserves another shot. And deserves someone who will listen to *why*."

Her eyes are watering. "All right now, you better get going. You tell that Martin McGee he needs to wake up."

......

Spitty, I'm serious. Something is different here. Heavier. I don't think I have time. I need you to sleep. Nap. Something.

How about this? I bet my life that you won't be able to dream of me before Petra.

37

Because it's Monday, the Believe Marty Can Fly team has dwindled. I can now identify almost everyone here: Mama Dorothy, Mr. McGee, Katie, her husband Rick, Turrey, Brooke, another boy that I think is the Chris I've heard mentioned a few times, and two older women that must be family as well. Real life must resume I know, but it still surprises me to find the waiting room so empty. The dozens of unfamiliar faces gone, back home to start their summer rituals once more.

As we walk in, everyone pastes on temporary happy faces. Turrey and Brooke stand up to give us hugs. I'm still coasting on autopilot. Too dazed to understand how this sequence of events continues to escalate. The four of us go to our usual spot. Whether it's a lunchroom or a waiting room, you make a choice once, and it becomes yours forevermore. We sit down, a collection of ninety-degree angles: perfect nervous posture.

Cameron wraps her arms around me. Daniel's body wash, some woodsy scent called Rustic Mist that we all scrubbed ourselves with this morning, wafts off her. It should smell the same as it does on me, yet somehow, it's more comforting. I breathe it in and exhale it out, pulling myself in closer to her to hold on to it. Cameron nuzzles me like a mother would, surrendering her personal space to my needs. "How are you not in the middle of some great life crisis like the rest of us?" I ask her.

"Being the mother hen to you dysfunctional chicks *is* my life crisis."

"I'm serious. It's come to my attention that I've missed quite a bit for the past year. I need to make sure you're okay too. It's not enough to just assume."

"I am. Swear."

I try to scrape off her neutral expression and see the truth beneath it. "You did borderline steal a wallet."

She flicks my wrist, nervous one of the adults overheard me. In her heart she knows, like I do, that everyone is far too distracted to eavesdrop on us. "Can I be honest with you?" she asks. I tilt my head up and give her a look that says *duh*, but I understand some stories require this kind of preface, even when being told to your best friend. "My parents pretty much want the opposite of what Aminah's and yours do. They're excited that I'm staying out all night and stuff because they're afraid I'm some kind of zombie with no real life outside of school. I mean, it's summer now, but you know what I mean."

"I do."

"They're sort of right. Aminah's sleeping on my floor and sneaking into her house to get things she needs. Daniel's having this sweeping love affair. You're some kind of mysterious dream communicator who skipped out on a final for an entire year then took it without studying and passed. I don't know how to be interesting in the midst of such interesting friends." She pauses. "I took the wallet so I could have a story to tell."

"Aw, Cam," Aminah says. She was eavesdropping. "You're the best slash most interesting human I know."

"I agree," I say. "I've never met a single other person with a self-made Art Garfunkel shirt, and if one other such person does exist, I'm positive they wouldn't wear it three days in a row just to be supportive."

"I've always loved the fact that you never really screw up," Daniel offers, also eavesdropping. "It makes me a little mad while also secretly inspires me to be better." He hugs us for a brief moment, then pulls us all apart. "Okay. Do me next!"

Aminah thwacks him with Cameron's magazine. "You're so humble, and you love sensitive moments," she starts. "You wish they could go on forever and ever. I love you, I love you, I love you, I love you—"

Daniel grabs her. "Ding ding ding! Time's up!"

Mama Dorothy comes over to us. She's carrying a container of food. "People won't stop bringing me stuff they made," she tells us as she starts handing out chocolate chip cookies. "I need to pawn it off on you kids." She pauses when she gets to me. "I tried to place you the other day, but I don't think you're the girl who broke out in hives at Marty's choir concert in sixth grade." She looks so inviting, even when bleary-eyed and distant, keeping her happy face plastered on to make everyone else feel better.

"Martin and I didn't go to the same grade school."

"Did he take you to a dance? I swear I know your face."

Her hand rubs my cheek so gently, so maternally, that I get up to hug her. "I met Martin at graduation."

"And you've been here all weekend? That's the sweetest thing." She starts to cry. Daniel grabs the cookie container from her hands so she can hug me tighter. We just hold each other, two almost strangers in the most personal of embraces. "What's your name?"

"I'm Petra," I say with a small laugh. Finally, I get to tell her my name.

"Petra," she repeats back. "Like the Metra."

Katie laughs. "That's totally a joke Marty would make."

Mama Dorothy pretends to fluff her hair, shaking her hips. "Where do you think he gets it from?"

"Mom, please stop," Katie says.

Mama Dorothy does one last shake. "All right, that's enough. I need to go see my boy. Who's coming with me?"

"I am," I say. It falls out of my mouth before I can consider it. This time around, it makes more sense for me to see him.

Martin McGee is not a stranger to me anymore.

"Let's get to it," Mama Dorothy says.

We walk down the hallway to those same doors I buzzed through on Saturday morning. Our hearts are heavy, but our heads are high, one foot in front of the other. The nurse lets us in, and we go to Martin's room. Right away I head straight to his bedside. Some of the swelling on his face has gone down, but he looks…distant. His haircut is already growing out a little, filling in those small patches I'd noticed on Saturday. No movement beneath his eyelids.

In my mind, I start a conversation with him. Maybe this is what it takes. Talking to him when I'm awake like I do when I'm asleep.

Hi, Martin, I start. I decide to fill him in on what I'm seeing. I don't know how any of this works. It's worth a try. Maybe he will be able to see it too. Or hear me.

Please hear me.

Your right eye is swollen shut, I continue. *It's bulbous and purple, like a baseball is caught underneath your skin. You have a tube in your throat. It's ugly and cruel, but it keeps you breathing because I guess you aren't doing it on your own. I'm hovering over you, examining the tiny details I promised myself on Saturday I wouldn't get to know. I'm double-checking them against the face I've come to know so well in my dreams.*

That little scar above your lip, on the left side, uncorrupted by the crash. When we danced, before I put my head back on your shoulder and that song we both knew but couldn't hear was on, I caught a glimpse of it there. I put my finger over it when I shushed you. It's an old scar, level with your skin, a little whiter than the rest. I want to know how you got it, Martin. I want you to tell me that, in your own words, in the here and now, not in some airplane I've created in my brain to have some great symbolism about the lack of control in my life or whatever.

You've seen my fears. Literally. And you keep showing up. You keep asking to be there. You held me so nicely when we danced, close, but not too close. Maybe we can do that in real life.

But it would have to be here, Martin.

I'm supposed to head off to college. It's really happening now. I passed my last exam. That's two months from now, though. Look how much we've accomplished in three days. In two months—wow— what could we do with two whole months? Even if it was here, you in the hospital relearning how to use your good hand or learning how to talk again or whatever it is you need to learn. I would help you. Whatever it takes.

But it would have to be here, Martin.

My pleas are probably so empty. Maybe I don't mean to you what you've come to mean to me. Maybe it's silly to make you mean so much, but somehow, you do. Maybe the you in my head isn't the one that's lying here on this hospital bed, but this voice deep inside of me tells me it is.

Earlier today, when I dreamed of us at your party, you started to say I'd shown you what there is to love about this place. I've been thinking about that. It's who you're with that makes a place great, you know? I have these fantastic friends. They've been with me every day since your accident happened. They are what make this ordinary town so extraordinary. I'd like you to meet them, like I've gotten to meet your friends. We all get along so well. You'd fit right in.

But it would have to be here, Martin.

I can't say any of these things aloud. Your mom, who is extraordinary too, I must say, is standing over my shoulder. I'm telling you here, in my mind. Isn't it amazing how full a mind is, all these deep, complex thoughts happening inside, when in reality, my body is just standing? Your body has betrayed you altogether, and yet I know your mind is still spinning. I know it.

It doesn't make sense.

It's been only three days, Martin. Such a short amount of time in the bigger picture. In the long, full life waiting for you on the other side of your eyelids. Just open them up and it's yours.

I don't know what else to say. All you have to do is open your eyes. Prove the doctors wrong. Doctors can be wrong. Life may seem like a science, but I'm learning that it's never black and white. Be the gray. Be the miracle. Whatever you want to call it.

Prove that kindness can be fairness.

Come back, Martin.

Please.

......

Don't do this to me, Petra. It's like I can feel you here, so close, hovering over me, listening to what I'm saying to Spitty, telling me to think this through. I have, Petra. I swear I have.

You reminded me to be patient, and that's the only reason I noticed this stuff in the first place. You don't understand what this is like.

I know. That's a cop-out. I've tried so many times now to explain it all the way, but all I ever say is that I'm stuck and I can't wake up and I need help. That's not deep enough. Have you ever really been stuck? Like, as a kid, did you ever get your head caught between the banisters of a staircase? Or climb all the way up a tree and look down, realizing you have no idea how to get back? You feel helpless. This place is like that times a billion.

I bet you're thinking that every person that's ever been stuck has managed to get out. I wish you'd seen *Back to the Future* because it would help me explain my point. Long story short, the main guy, Marty McFly, gets stuck in 1955, and his mom kind of falls in love with him. I know that sounds wild, but you gotta watch it. Anyway, spoiler alert, he gets back to the time he's from by the end, which isn't that bad of a spoiler because I doubt it would be such a universally loved movie if he didn't.

I'm telling you about it because he got back with the help of this guy, Doc, like you'd get your head out of the banisters with the help of a parent or—in my case—an EMT with a saw. You'd get out of the tree with the help of a parent, or—in my case— Spitty with a mattress. There isn't anyone here, Petra. It's just me and my mind. There's no one to help me out of the quicksand. You saved me from sinking down farther, from losing myself, but I'm the one that has to do the rest. Helping Spitty let go of that memory dream is my way out. I'm Doc. He's Marty. I'm the mattress. He's the kid in the tree. You see? I can set him free, Petra, so don't you dare go to sleep and dream of me first. I don't want to hear it.

You're already so close. I know it. It's like I can feel your breath on my face.

......

"Doesn't it seem like if you get close enough, you'll wake him up?" Mama Dorothy asks.

I jerk up. I'd been trying so hard to send Martin my message that I'd been leaning closer and closer until the space between us could be measured in inches, and I didn't even realize. "Yeah, it really does."

Dorothy strokes Martin's head. "It hasn't worked for me yet, but I keep trying."

"So," I start, holding out the *o*.

"Unplug one and it's done, apparently. It's my call." She grabs my hand and squeezes tight, kissing my knuckles.

It doesn't seem right. Bodies function every day without any thought. It's all automatic. Breathing, speaking, sitting, standing. Even if I tried to think about it, stop myself from breathing, the breath itself would win eventually. I wish that would happen for Martin too. It's so unfair.

There's that word again. *Fair.*

A tear falls down my cheek onto my hand interlaced with Mama Dorothy's. "Please don't cry. You'll get me going again."

"I'm sorry. This must be so impossible for you. I hardly know him, and I feel this way. You—" I stop myself. "You."

"Hey, it's not about how long you've known someone. It's about what you give them," she says. She wipes a tear off my cheek. "Besides, moms are made of steel. We have to be. I'm thinking of this round as nothing but another one of his little tests."

There's a knock at the door. It's Mr. McGee. Everyone else from the waiting room crowds behind him.

"Didn't the nurse say two at a time?" Mama Dorothy asks.

"Yeah, well, you know teenagers," Mr. McGee says. "The nurse buzzed the door open for me, and they all followed."

Mama Dorothy gestures everyone toward us. "All of you hurry in here before someone comes to yell at us."

The whole group files into the room. We stand shoulder to shoulder, like a pack of commuters snuggled together on the train in winter. Someone, the boy who must be Chris, closes the door, and the room becomes beeping machines and shuffling feet, everyone in a constant state of readjustment. For some, like Daniel, Cameron, and Aminah, this is their first time seeing Martin like this, and the reality of it paints their faces into sinking, sagging, sad portraits. It's almost electric in here. Tears and desperate breaths. Whispered words. Wringing hands.

A synthesizer?

It's quiet at first, a hand covering the sound. The hand moves away, and I comprehend what I'm hearing—the first few chords of "Jump." Mr. McGee has his phone held up above his head.

"This one's for you, Marty," he says. The volume's still too soft, but it doesn't matter. We all know it. A foot starts stomping. A hand claps the beat. My voice hums the shrieking opening notes. The vocals come in, and in unison, we sing. Then there's mumbling, some people knowing the words—the McGees and the older ladies, us kids faking it along—until we get to the chorus. All at once when Van Halen commands it, we do it. We jump.

The room shakes. A nurse immediately opens the door. "What in the—?" she starts. "There's way too many of you in here!"

"Please," Turrey begs, putting his smooth-talking confidence to good use. "We'll be quieter."

She rolls her eyes. "Five minutes," she warns.

"Jump!" we shout when she leaves.

38

In a lot so packed cars are double-parked, Spencer still got his designated spot. As he walks up to his beautiful color-inverted orca of a Caravan, he can't help but smile over all his good fortune. He got great parking. He got his last in-school suspension waived. He graduated high school.

He climbs into the driver's seat of the White Whale. Fly rides shotgun. Neither has removed their robes, even though it's hot as hell outside and Spencer hates his. Stronger than the hate is the love for what it represents—one last middle finger to the schooling system. Nobody can tell Spencer when he can or cannot leave his own graduation. To prove a point, he'll be a yellow-clad rebel in a van made for a soccer mom with his best friend by his side doing the same.

Spencer takes the whiskey bottles out of the glove compartment. He's already feeling woozy from the two he chugged before the ceremony and the one he drank with Fly behind the bleachers. He hands a bottle to Fly and takes the other for himself. The liquor burns less this time around, which is good, because he can chug it faster. Nothing is better to Spencer than having Fly do this with him. Stand by his side as he waves the black flag.

"You did it," Fly says. "You got me first." He looks so happy. Just like he should be. But he hasn't touched his whiskey.

"You gonna have that?" Spencer asks.

"Nah," Fly answers. "Don't need it."

The Caravan revs up with ease. Spencer throws it into drive. Windows down. Warm air. Their town flies by, each passing foot of distance traveled both familiar and brand-new. All of it perfect.

"I used to think I hated this place," Fly says. "Now I know that I wouldn't be me without it. I'd have different friends, probably different nicknames. A whole different life." He tickles the outside air with his fingers. "And I wouldn't want that."

Spencer presses his foot harder into the pedal. The White Whale screeches along, trying to satisfy his need for speed and take him into the magical, unidentified something he's convinced waits for him on the other side of this momentous occasion.

When he looks to see Fly's reaction, he finds Fly smiling like he's got a secret. "We had it good, Spitty. Really good." Fly looks at Spencer. Right in his eyes. "By the way, there's a car coming."

It's nothing but a flicker. A black hole growing by the millisecond, ready to devour them whole. Fly pulls his hand back in from the window and tugs the steering wheel to the left. "Don't hit the brakes!" he calls out.

That's right. That black dot is not a gigantic bug or a huge bird or an enormous piece of dirt. It's an old black Pontiac Grand Am driving steadily along, the man behind the wheel not wearing sunglasses or a seat belt, unable to see the giant white van headed straight for the center of the intersection.

"Fly! Look out! Look out!"

The car doesn't stop. Neither does the Caravan. Spencer's foot doesn't find the brake pedal. They make it across the intersection without a collision, veered so far over they're in the oncoming traffic lane. Fly corrects the steering wheel, and Spencer lays off the gas, easing onto the brake until the White Whale comes to a puttering stop.

"It worked!" Fly yells.

Spencer pulls his palms to his mouth for a series of screams, needing to release all the pent-up adrenaline of the almost accident. When his tirade runs its course and every curse word has been cursed, he unbuckles himself to get some air. He gets out of the car and walks past the driver's back seat, staring at his shoes, trying to shake the persistent fear out of his tensed limbs. Beneath his feet, he notices debris. Small, indeterminate chunks of plastic and metal and glass. He looks up.

The scene of the crime roars to life. The Grand Am is pushed away from the Caravan, but the front hood is so scrunched up it looks like an accordion. That would be horrific enough on its own, but what lies on top of the scrunched hood is so unfathomable that Spencer starts heaving up all of the whiskey and some of the cereal he scarfed down this morning. His tender ribs make the whole process hurt so much he fears he might pass out, but he's incapable of stopping. He empties his stomach, and when nothing but clear spit comes up, he uncurls himself to look again, clutching his broken ribs. Because they *are* broken. It doesn't matter that Fly moved the wheel and the Grand Am didn't hit them in the dream.

That doesn't change what happened in reality.

The front windshield of the Grand Am is shattered, leaving only a jagged outline around the periphery. Most of the glass has ended up on the ground, mixed in with a liquid that's not quite red. More like cherry-tinged chocolate sauce. The source of it, stretched out like Superman attempting to fly into a wall, is a mangled body, the head of which is turned at such an unnatural angle that it's facing skyward. Spencer can't help it. He retches up more clear spit.

The passenger door of the White Whale opens. "Holy shit," Fly says. He can't take his eyes off the wreckage. Once he steps far enough away from the van, it twists and crumbles into its proper form. "I didn't even think about the other car."

"He's dead," Spencer says, pointing to the lifeless man. "I killed him."

"That's what Petra meant," Fly mutters. He shoots a look to Spencer. "I can't change this."

"I killed him," Spencer repeats.

Fly grabs Spencer's shoulders, shaking him. "Don't do this. It's not your fau…well, it's not *just* your…you made a mistake, but so did I."

"I killed him." Suddenly, Spencer remembers the rest. The way it really happened. "And I killed you too."

"No. Spencer. No. I swear on—on—on—my shoe collection that you didn't. That was a pathetic thing to say. I don't know what to say. Shit."

"You told Petra about the pact. You knew you would die."

"I thought this would be easier. I'm only making a bigger mess. I wanted to set you free of this."

"What do I have?" Spencer asks. "Nothing. My car is totaled. Everyone hates me. As they should. I killed someone. He's dead. Right there. And I killed you. I know I did."

Spencer starts wailing. His cries are loud and ugly, so invasive that Fly shudders.

"This happened!" Spencer screams. "It's not a dream. It's reality. You're not supposed to be walking. You're supposed to look like—"

He stops, thinking it instead of saying it, using his memory to change Fly's body into how it was after the real crash. Fly's entire right side crunches and curls, not hurting him physically, only altering his appearance.

"Look at yourself!" Spencer screams. Fly checks his reflection against the side of the van. "That's what I see! That's what I *did*! It's not okay. It won't get easier. How could you say that?"

"Spitty, I'm sorry! I wanted to make it better."

"It's not. It won't be." Spencer looks at the body on the car. "I caused this. I bought the whiskey. I told you to leave early. I drove too fast. You can't change any of it."

"Shit," Fly whispers.

"Whether you live or you die, this is what it is for me. This is what I have," Spencer says. He falls to his knees, then sits back, staring at the scene of the crime. "If anything, you made it worse. You made me relive this part."

Fly wraps his arms around Spencer. "I'm sorry," he whispers, but it isn't enough.

Nothing ever will be.

PART FIVE

39

Aminah gives me shotgun. Daniel turns the air vents so they're facing me. Cameron pats my head from the back seat. And the Prius does what it always does, takes us where we need to go without complaint. It's stunning outside. Picturesque in a surreal way, like the sun has managed to crack everything open and make it sparkle. Trees shimmer in the unyielding light, dripping leaves. There are no shades in the sky, no varying levels—it's as pure a blue as a child's crayon portrait of the perfect day.

"Which one is it?" Daniel asks as he turns down the cul-de-sac.

"Orange one with the basketball hoop. You can't miss it."

"That's right," he remembers. We can see it from the start of the block. Cars are everywhere, parallel parked on both sides of the street. "Looks like we'll be walking." We follow the curve of the cul-de-sac and go back out onto the perpendicular street, driving a full block and a half before we find an open spot.

"You forgot your coffee back at your house," Aminah notices.

"It's okay. I had some before you guys picked me up," I tell her.

"There's a little left of mine, if you want some. It's in the cup holder back here."

"Mine too," Cameron adds. "But I know you don't like my sugary drinks."

"I do though," Daniel says with a smirk.

"No way. Sorry I don't punish myself with plain iced coffee like *some people*." She catches Daniel's eye in the rearview mirror to give him a pointed look.

"You guys really don't have to be so accommodating to me," I interrupt.

Daniel starts parallel parking. "This is not accommodation. It's kindness. Mine expires in twenty-four hours, so you better use it up. It's the best Groupon deal you'll ever get."

I clutch the door handle as he cuts into the tight space. He comes inches from grazing the car to our right, but he makes it work.

"I'm not the only one going through it, though," I counter.

"But you're the reason we're here, so you get the love today, kid." Daniel opens his door and gets out. He fixes his black dress shirt in the window, the same one he wore to prom. Prom— three weeks or a trillion years ago.

"Accept it. It's how it has to be. Next week, you can take me to get my car washed or something. Right now, you're ours to watch over."

The rest of us get out and begin our walk to Martin's house. When we turn down his cul-de-sac, the sound of conversation is so loud it's like we're entering a festival.

In a weird way, we are.

So many people are everywhere, on the lawn, in the open garage, bleeding out onto the sidewalks, all different ages and varying energies: some more formal in their dark ensembles, others casual, some bold enough to wear bright colors. I know faces now from the other weekend—shuffling in and out of the waiting room. Daniel, on the other hand, knows their names, and as we pass by, he shares anecdotes. It's what he's always done, tell us stories about the strangers we call classmates. I never really listened before. Now I find myself wondering who might've been my friend. Whose path might cross with mine still. What spaces in my life I've yet to notice.

Martin... Are you here?

Brooke finds us first. She's woven dark red flowers into the intricate bun on the side of her head. "Thank you," she says as she hugs me.

"For what?" I ask, even though I know where this is going. A twinge of jealousy pinches my face into something like a grimace. I do my best to mask it before she answers, forcing myself to lift the corners of my mouth into a smile.

"I've had so many dreams of him. I know he's really there watching over me. All of us."

She's not the first person to have told me this. In fact, almost all of my friends, new and old, have talked to me about seeing Martin in their dreams this past week.

"I like that," I say. Because I do. It's been a rough seven days. The victories are worth celebrating, even if I can't share in them.

Where are you, Martin?

"Do you guys want any food?" Brooke asks. "My abuela made these amazing empanadas. Come on. I'll show you."

We form a line behind her, grabbing one another by the fabric of our clothing to stay together. That's how packed it is. But the crowd tapers out as we go down into the basement. This is where a lot of the food is being kept, spread out on a pool table.

I know this pool table, I realize.

And I know this basement.

Here I am, a place I've never been, and yet it lived in my mind before I ever saw it with my eyes. *You were right, Martin. I got the couch wrong.* It's a little yellower and patchier. But this pool table is just right. So right my eyes water at the sight of it, and I have to look down at my nails. I start picking off the polish.

"They're all stuffed with different fillings," Brooke tells us. "I made little labels that say what's in them in case you have allergies or whatever. Or you hate cilantro," she says, poking Daniel.

The others grab plates and make their choices. I'm not hungry yet. Cameron places a hand on my back to guide me toward the sectional.

Are you seeing this, Martin? Are you watching us right now?

"Is Turrey coming?" Brooke asks Daniel.

"He's on his way. Martin's mom asked him to pick up some more ice."

Brooke busts out into a huge grin.

"What?" Daniel asks.

Brooke keeps grinning.

"Ugh, yes, we're officially dating now, if you *must* know," he tells her.

"I didn't say anything!" she protests.

"Your face said everything."

"I'm happy for you." She sets her plate on her lap. "And it's nice to feel happy for people right now."

Everyone starts eating. "You were right. Your abuela is an amazing cook," Daniel admits to Brooke.

My mouth waters at the sight of the empanadas. They look flaky and melty and perfect. I excuse myself to get up and get one after all. I walk around the back of the couch, stopping in the place where we last spoke.

You and I stood right here. There was some cake on the tip of your nose. I never told you that. It made you seem young and happy. I liked it that way.

Everyone else has updated me on you since then. Turrey texted yesterday to tell me you and him went to a diner and ate ham steaks together. Katie said you guys threw out the first pitch at a Cubs game together. Even Cameron has seen you. She said she was five again, and you were there watching her piano recital. When she finished, you convinced everyone to give her a standing ovation for her rendition of "Hot Cross Buns."

I'm trying not to take it personally, but it does seem strange. For three days, I couldn't close my eyes without running into you, and at that time, I had the luxury of being able to open them and see you in real life too. Now I don't have either. And if I'm being honest, it sucks. A lot. But I have to rally. Your mom said no tears were to be shed today. I gave her your letter at the funeral. She turned around and planned this party. It's supposed to be a celebration of your life, like you wanted. So if you're looking at me right now, look away for a second. I'm going to wipe my eyes, then I'll sit back down and enjoy this moment. Make a good reason and all that. I know that's what you'd want. I literally know, since you said it to me.

When I walked in today, I overheard your friend Chris telling a group of people that Katie waxed your eyebrows in seventh grade. That made everyone laugh.

We're all doing it for you. We're trying to smile and be happy and remember the good.

For a long time, I thought of myself as falling, but because of you, I realized I've been climbing. White-knuckle clinging to the edge of myself, working my way up to the light, inch by inch, finding joy where it seems there is none. Trying to stay focused on that instead of staring at the dark of my past. It's hard, but it's worth it. I've even learned to do it in my dreams. Ryan doesn't show up anymore.

Then again, neither do you.

"Petra?" Aminah turns to look at me. "What are you doing?"

God. I'm standing here staring like I'm in a trance. I don't explain myself to her. I get my empanada and come back to the couch. When I sit down, she hugs me. I love these people for holding me up as I, in unpredictable patterns, laugh and cry and sigh my way through this life.

We catch one another up on what's going on for the rest of

summer. We all have official plans now. Even Aminah. You gave her the courage to talk to her parents. She lives with them again. She's going to take the year off then reevaluate the possibility of school. I'm trying to convince her to go to Notre Dame with me. Isn't it weird you did that? You never even met her, and because of what happened to you, she made a change for the better.

I'm talking to my parents too. I found the courage to tell them what really happened to me. What Ryan did. They believe me, which means more than I knew it would. And they're encouraging me to speak up, so that he never does this to another girl again. I'm working on being brave enough to do just that. We're starting counseling next week. But now's not the time for that whole story.

This day is about you.

"What's up?" Turrey asks as he walks down the stairs, cool and confident as ever. Without hesitation, he takes the spot between Daniel and me. He gives Daniel a kiss and grabs his hand.

After a moment, he grabs my hand too.

This gesture, as small as it is, feels bigger than us. We are forever linked by what we've been through. One weekend that lasted longer than all of high school. I grab for Aminah. An unspoken ripple effect begins, and she grabs for Brooke, who grabs for Cameron, who moves herself off the couch to close this little circle. Once united, we stand up and bow forward, leaning in so our foreheads touch, a prayer for you pulsing through our fingertips.

"To Fly," Turrey says.

"To Fly," we repeat.

It falls silent again, our prayers continuing on in squeezes and breaths, memories spoken only in the mind, just for you to hear. As I look at the heads dropped down in this imperfect huddle, I realize you live inside our circle now, Martin. Forever you're the space between. The voice that floats into our heads when we need it most. The air that fills our lungs when it feels like breathing is too much. The ground that steadies us when our legs want to give out. Our best companion on the other side of waking life.

You're not stuck anymore, Martin.

You're free.

40

I t's a hot day in mid-June, humid and unforgiving. Yellow sunlight beams down on hundreds of heads haloed in yellow caps. What a powerful color yellow can be in mass quantity. It screams to be noticed. It begs for a smile. Petra obliges because she made it to the finish line. The diploma's in the mail. She passed the Honors Algebra II exam. She's graduating high school.

Just graduating.

Steve Taggart stands on the stage giving the valedictorian speech he's prepared for his whole life. Something about birds taking flight. It doesn't matter. Petra's not really listening because Steve's not really talking. He's nothing but a golden flicker of a distant memory. The last part of the last time anything was ever the same. He may as well be a mirage. Some far-off goal that keeps moving out of reach when you try to get closer.

For now, for this, Petra's content keeping her distance.

"You know, I've felt like a lot of things since this day, but never a bird. Sorry, Stevey." Sitting next to Petra, elbow pressed gently into her rib cage, graduation gown crumpled underneath his plastic chair but cap still on his head, is Martin. "Hate the robe, but I can't lie, I'm into the cap." He tips it in her direction.

"You're here," Petra marvels.

Sunlight doesn't wash out his face like it should. It holds back to let Petra see him. The yellow of her gown strengthens the deep amber around the rims of his pupils. So bright and alive he looks, all yellow himself, his huge smile beaming at her, reaching out like hands to pinch her cheeks back into her own version of uncensored happiness.

"Hope you don't have anywhere to be," he says. "I'd like to steal a tiny slice of your forever tonight. Today. You get it."

"This is just a dream, isn't it?" Petra realizes.

"Only if you want it to be."

Petra nods. It doesn't matter that she knows graduation happened ten days ago, and Martin died, and she went to his party today, and this is all in her mind. What happens in sleep can be as real as what happens when awake.

Her hand grazes Martin's. He takes the cue and grabs on. Their fingers lace together so neatly, the promise of stories yet untold woven into a tight bundle between them. Martin's pulse, so alive, beats into the top of her hand through his fingertips, thumping into her bloodstream.

"I've been waiting for this moment," Petra says. "You didn't make it easy."

He squeezes her hand tighter. "I'm sorry."

"Me too."

"No. You did everything you could. More than you should have. I get the only apology."

"Martin?"

"Yeah."

"That's not what I'm sorry for anymore. I'm sorry I never really got to know you."

"Petra?"

"Yeah."

"I like when you call me Martin."

Flushed, Petra turns away. Endless rows of empty white chairs surround her. The rest of her class has disappeared, but she isn't alone. She can still feel Martin's pulse against her own, syncopated beats married through their hands. Still the yellow remains. Softer now. It's not so hot. It's weather that isn't even weather anymore—a perfect, pleasant evenness that envelops everything.

"You're funny," Petra says.

Martin makes a fist with his free hand and pulls a victory arm pump into his chest. "I've been waiting my whole life to hear you say that."

Petra rolls her eyes. "Too far." Because he's gone, she remembers again. It's so easy to forget because it matters so little. Not at all actually. It doesn't have to matter here. This can be anywhere. They can do anything. But they don't want to. All they need is this very moment on their football field. The beginning of it all.

Petra's been choosing to look away from Martin, an old

nervous habit and a mistake she is quick to correct. When she turns to see him, nervousness is etched into his forehead: tiny taut wrinkles from where he holds tension.

"Sorry if my hand is sweaty," he says.

"It's perfect." Her heart rate skyrockets. It's her hand that's sweaty. It's she who is nervous. When he smiles, his scar, a little whiter than the rest, pulls wider. "How'd you get that?" she asks.

Martin knows what she means. "Wrestling in my backyard with Spitty."

"Figures."

"We were losers."

"I know."

"Then what are you sorry for? Sounds like you know all there is to know about me."

Petra exhales. Her features pull downward, trying to see in Martin's face how all of this ends. "What now?"

"Anything. Everything. Nothing. It's all possible."

"I mean when I wake up. You won't be there. And it's taken you so long to come here in the first place."

"I know," he says. "I was afraid."

"Of what?"

"You being mad at me."

Petra has to laugh. "You were afraid I'd be mad at you... for dying?"

"I didn't keep my end of the promise."

"Do you really think you had control over what was going to happen to you? I mean, a car hit you," she says softly. "There wasn't a way for you to change the outcome of that, no matter what you were doing in people's dreams."

"Dammit you're smart," he says. He pauses to think. His mood changes. "Can you tell my family I'm sorry? And the family of that other driver?"

Petra puts her other hand atop his leg. "Your mom set up a memorial in his name."

"Wow." He takes it in. "I didn't know that. When I visit them, it's not like it is with you. We don't talk about real stuff. It's just happiness. Memories. Lots of hugging." He fakes a shudder. "You can't believe the amount of hugging."

"You're a pretty huggable guy."

"You don't have to tell me twice."

Petra leans her head onto his shoulder. She can hear Martin breathing, full and real, his thoughts turning, his tongue untwisting, so used to saying the wrong thing and so eager to find the right thing. "This right here," he starts, "is what could have been in your world, and what is in mine. It's the place where we exist, together, exactly as we want to be."

Yes, she thinks to herself. *It is.*

Sunlight stretches their shadows onto the grass in front of them. There are no more chairs around. Smack-dab in the middle of the field with black outlines looming like giants, Petra and Martin continue talking. And laughing. And nudging each other. The fastest of friends in the brightest of lights, glowing for an imaginary amount of hours on a clock that does not move. Their shadow selves, like a mirror of yet another world, dance together.

This, Petra thinks, is the place where lost things are found. Where time doesn't matter. Where all of us live as our truest selves, in infinite forms, in moldable shapes. Where we shed our skin and become reborn, over and over, night after night, preparing ourselves for the hours that wait on the other side.

Acknowledgments

First and foremost, this book would not exist without my sister Rose. She's read every draft, supported every good idea, and talked me out of every bad one. Rose, I owe so much to your fervor and your keen eye. You are truly the most essential piece of my writerly puzzle. Thank you.

Mom, thank you for always cheering me on with unapologetic favoritism and bias. Every time I fall down, your love makes a mighty soft cushion. Dad, thank you for the daily phone calls. They mean everything and more. Liz, thank you for always being like a second mom to me. I live a fulfilling life as an adult because you selflessly invested your time and money into my interests when I was young. John and Raina, thank you for showing me how to be strong and lead with love. My nieces and nephews: Deklin, Brielle, Caleb, Brannon, Lily, Emma, and Sophie, thank you for making me so excited for the next generation. You guys are going to change the world for the better.

My amazing agent and ultimate cheerleader, Taylor Haggerty, thank you for connecting to this story in a way I could only—pun intended—dream of. Your relentless efforts made every facet of that dream a reality. You are a serious rock star. All those who know you adore you as much I do.

Annie Berger, my incredible editor, thank you for nurturing my book until it grew into something so much greater than I ever could've imagined alone. Your insight, expertise, kindness, and enthusiasm made the editing process much more enjoyable than it had any right to be. Huge thank-yous to Sarah Kasman, Cassie Gutman, Sandra Ogle, Nicole Hower, Jillian Rahn, Alex Yeadon, Katy Lynch, the rest of the Sourcebooks team, and every other person who helped me make this book a reality. I would like to tackle hug and high-five all of you.

Ryan Salonen, thank you for your investment in my work and for making me believe all my ideas are worthy of exploration. Your encouragement has helped me overcome countless obstacles. Vince Rossi, thank you for always having an unending passion for the creative arts. Your fervor makes the stars seem reachable. Brian Batty, thank you for giving Martin his shoes and for giving me endless reasons to laugh. This book will always be Fist Bump to us, with music provided by Bottle Cap Effect. Ryan Everett, thank you for never ceasing to turn every morning into a perfect one. In so many ways, you make me brighter. Hollis Andrews, thank you for hyping me up every chance you get. Four hands on the wheel! To all the other friends who have hugged me, smiled with me, cried with me, distracted me, enlightened me, and supported me throughout this process: please know that you live inside every word I write. Our memories are magic.

All my gratitude to Oak Forest High School's Cheryl Harris-Sumida and Victor Pazik, my former drama director and choir director, respectively. You both shaped my life's path in ways too big to be qualified. You gave my hopes and ambitions a safe space to grow. You two are superheroes in my eyes.

Thank you to each and every one of the gymnasts I've worked with over the past decade. It's an honor to share this amazing sport with all of you. To my LGA Xcel team especially, every day you girls show me there is no goal that can't be reached if you love what you do and you're willing to put in the work. Your determination and heart will take you far in life. I am so proud to be your coach.

To the Chicago Cubs, baseball team of my heart, thank you for finally winning it all. You changed so many lives for the better on November 2, 2016.

Finally, to all the YA lovers out there, thank you for celebrating books as you do. I carry a permanent swell of affection for each and every one of you, akin to the heart-hugging squeeze that comes along when I'm reading a really good book. You know the feeling.

About the Author

Bridget Morrissey lives in Los Angeles, but proudly hails from Oak Forest, Illinois, a small yet mighty suburb just southwest of Chicago. When she's not writing, she can be found coaching gymnastics, reading in the corner of a coffee shop, or headlining concerts in her living room. Visit her online at bridgetjmorrissey.com.